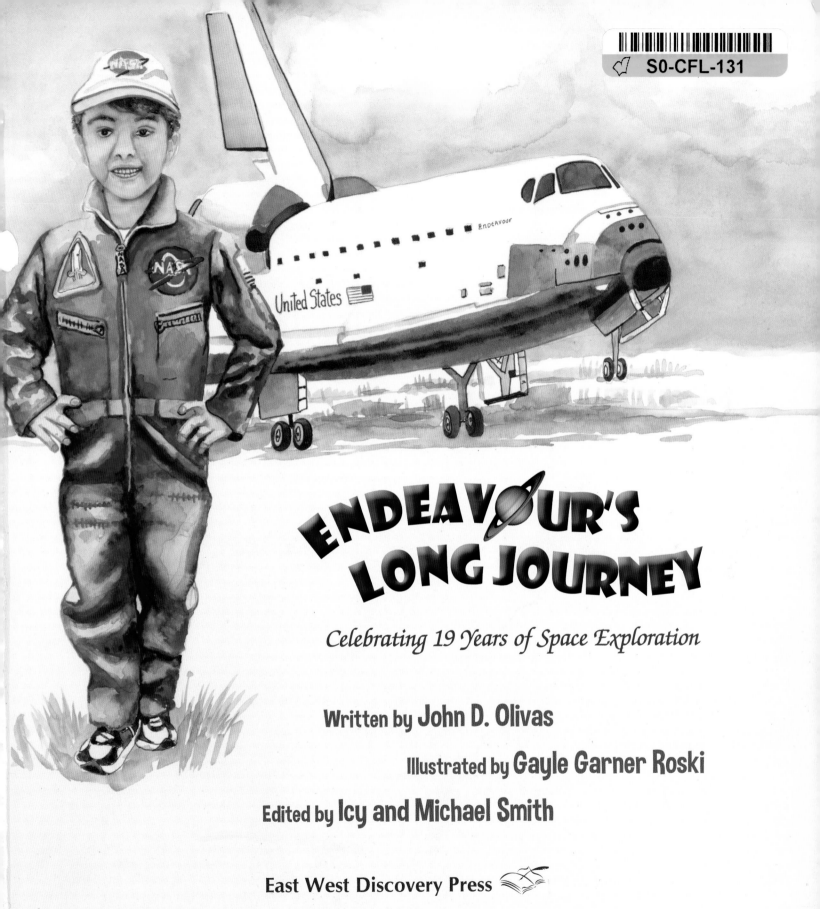

ENDEAVOUR'S LONG JOURNEY

Celebrating 19 Years of Space Exploration

Written by **John D. Olivas**

Illustrated by **Gayle Garner Roski**

Edited by **Icy and Michael Smith**

East West Discovery Press

Manhattan Beach, CA

Text copyright © 2013 by East West Discovery Press
Illustrations copyright © 2013 by Gayle Garner Roski
Introductory Statement by Charles F. Bolden Jr. is a Work of the U.S. Government.

Published by:
East West Discovery Press
P.O. Box 3585, Manhattan Beach, CA 90266
Phone: 310-545-3730, Fax: 310-545-3731
Website: www.eastwestdiscovery.com

Written by John D. Olivas
Illustrated by Gayle Garner Roski
Edited by Icy Smith and Michael Smith
Design and production by Jennifer Thomas and Icy Smith
Photo research by Icy Smith
Photo credits: p. 30, *Endeavour* being towed down the street by Jennifer Thomas; p. 37, *Endeavour* exhibit display by Michael Smith; all other photos courtesy of NASA.

Library of Congress Cataloging-in-Publication Data

Olivas, John D.
Endeavour's long journey : celebrating 19 years of space exploration / written by John D. Olivas ; edited by Icy and Michael Smith ; illustrated by Gayle Garner Roski ; [photos, NASA].
p. cm. -- (Space exploration series)
Summary: While visiting the science museum with his mother and sister, Jojo finds himself on a journey through space as the retired space shuttle Endeavour describes her missions and the people involved. Includes "fun facts" about Endeavour, "famous firsts" of five space shuttles, quizzes, and a glossary.
Includes bibliographical references and index.
ISBN 978-0-9856237-2-2 (hardcover : alk. paper) -- ISBN 978-0-9856237-3-9 (pbk) 1. Endeavour (Space shuttle)--Juvenile fiction. [1. Endeavour (Space shuttle)--Fiction. 2. Manned space flight--Fiction. 3. Extravehicular activity (Manned space flight)--Fiction. 4. United States. National Aeronautics and Space Administration--Fiction.] I. Roski, Gayle Garner, ill. II. United States. National Aeronautics and Space Administration. III. Title.

PZ7.O46828End 2013
[Fic]--dc23

2012040567

ISBN-13: 978-0-9856237-2-2 Hardcover
ISBN-13: 978-0-9856237-3-9 Paperback
Printed in China
Published in the United States of America

To my children, Isabella, James, Anthony, Joseph, and Gabrielle.
Look to the heavens and become all that you can be.

—J. D. O.

To my granddaughter, Charlotte Alivia Pearl.
I cherish our morning walks, which happen most every day.
And soon, like going to outer space, she'll be up, up and away.

—G. G. R.

*The publisher extends special thanks to
Nicholas Fansmith for his assistance
in bringing the main character, Jo Jo, to life.*

FOREWORD

When I was seven years old, my father took me to the Hayden Planetarium in New York City. I saw telescopes, pictures of the planets, images of the stars in the heavens, and actual meteorites that had fallen to earth. It was fascinating, and on the ride back home I told my father I wanted to become an engineer and design rocket ships that would someday take astronauts to space. Recognizing my interest in science, space, and the quest for knowledge, my father took me to the library and introduced me to a wide variety of books. After school I would read as many books as time would allow to learn about science, great people, and how to build things like model planes that I could actually fly. Those studies grew and continued even as an adult. Eventually I graduated from college and accepted a job at National Aeronautics and Space Administration (NASA). After many years of designing and managing spacecraft projects at NASA and later at a private corporation, the President of the United States asked me to become the director of America's Space Program as the Administrator of NASA. It was a dream come true for me, which started with my father taking me on a trip to a museum and exposing me to good books.

Books like *Endeavour's Long Journey* are important to inspire young people like you to think about mathematics, science, and technology in a fun way. It may lead to a fantastic career like I have had, whether becoming an engineer, an astronaut, or even the director of NASA. This story demonstrates how a very diverse group of hard-working people worked together to accomplish important and difficult tasks. We should all strive to make a difference as individuals. And as we do, we can help change the world for the better.

Daniel Saul Goldin
9th Administrator of NASA
April 1, 1992 – May 21, 2001

INTRODUCTORY STATEMENT

Growing up as an African American in Columbia, South Carolina, in the segregated South, I never dreamed of becoming a pilot and especially not an astronaut. My mom and dad were both schoolteachers and they always told me that I could do anything I wanted if I studied hard, dreamed big, and never let anyone tell me what I could and couldn't do. With the encouragement and support of my parents, I studied very hard to get into the United States Naval Academy and graduated to become a United States Marine Corps Officer and pilot—later a Naval Test Pilot. But in spite of their urging to reach for the stars with my dreams, it was not until I met and talked with the late Dr. Ron McNair, also an African American from South Carolina and a member of the first group of NASA astronauts selected in 1978 to fly the Space Shuttle, that I decided to apply for the Shuttle Program. Ron told me much the same as Jojo is told by *Endeavour* in the book: "Dream your dreams, and make them happen." With Ron's mentorship, I did become an astronaut and flew the Shuttle four times into space, commanding two of my missions. Being part of the Space Shuttle Program was an exciting and rewarding part of my 34-year Marine Corps career. The Shuttle Program brought critical diversity to the human spaceflight program, as from that first class in 1978 to today, it has included people from many races, cultures, nations, and religions as well as very diverse technical backgrounds. Young boys and girls everywhere are inspired by information on space flight and the orbital vehicles that were part of the Space Shuttle Program's phenomenal 30-year era.

Charles F. Bolden Jr.
12th Administrator of NASA

"We're going to the science center!" I scream with excitement.

We have been there before, but my sister, Bella, was very little then. I remember pretending to be a pilot in the cool planes they have out front.

"Today is going to be extra special," Mom tells us. "Do you remember watching television, seeing the space shuttle *Endeavour* flying across the country on the back of another aircraft? She and the other shuttles were a very important part of human exploration of space. She has journeyed a long, long way."

As we arrive, hundreds of people walk toward the museum. We wonder what *Endeavour* will look like up close.

"Mom, why do you keep calling *Endeavour* a 'she'?" I ask.

"Well Jojo, it's simple. Just like I take care of you and your sister, *Endeavour* took care of all the astronauts who flew her. The astronauts think of *Endeavour* kind of like their mother. They really do. And the astronauts treat her with great care and also respect, as they depend on her."

As we walk under *Endeavour's* wings, we can see the many heat shield tiles that protect her from the high temperatures generated when re-entering Earth's atmosphere from space. She is magnificent. Everyone is "oohing" and "ahhing."

I dream about how this enormous shuttle has carried astronauts, and I wonder what it would have been like to be part of the crew—to eat, sleep, and work inside.

Suddenly, I feel myself floating...

United States

Then, a soft voice whispers, "Thanks for your visit, Jojo."

What is that? I ask myself.

"It's me, *Endeavour*!" Her voice is kind and gentle, but firm—like Mom's. "Come join me on the journey I have traveled."

I look at my clothes—now a blue flight suit, the kind astronauts wear! Then the world begins to fade.

All that is left is *Endeavour* and me. It is pitch black with millions of stars, and Earth is far below. But I'm not afraid. Floating in space is fun! Now I know what it feels like to be in microgravity.

Gravity

The further away from Earth you are, the less and less pull there is of the Earth's gravity. To feel almost no gravity, you would have to be almost to the Moon, over 200,000 miles away. However, the shuttle never travels that far from the planet, only about 300 miles up. The gravity that high is actually still very close to here on Earth. Astronauts float for a different reason. In order to avoid falling back to Earth, the shuttle goes around the Earth very fast. Like going fast on a playground merry-go-round, you are pulled away from the center.

The shuttle travels about 17,500 miles an hour around Earth. Even though the shuttle is being pulled back toward Earth by gravity, it is traveling so fast and so high, it is actually falling around the Earth. This is known as microgravity. Since the shuttle and its astronauts are actually falling around the Earth, they float together in orbit. When the shuttle is ready to come home, it simply slows down and falls back to Earth.

Next, I find myself inside *Endeavour*, on the flight deck. I look at the instrument panel, which shows we are traveling at 17,500 miles per hour! "That's how fast we need to travel to stay in orbit," she says.

"Wow!" I am amazed.

"But getting into space is just the start. This was my first mission," *Endeavour* explains. I watch the astronauts on the mid-deck, frantically preparing for an urgent situation. A satellite that has been launched into space is not working properly. The astronauts need to perform a spacewalk to grab the satellite and bring it back to Earth.

"It was a dangerous mission. This was the very first and only time that three spacewalkers left the ship at the same time. They actually captured the satellite with their hands.

"The air lock in the mid-deck allowed the astronauts to leave their comfy crew compartment for the potential danger outside," she adds. "And they used a very special spacesuit to do this. In space, the temperature can reach 200 degrees Fahrenheit in the sun, and minus 200 degrees Fahrenheit in the shade.

"The suits also help the astronauts to breathe. There is no air in space, so if anything happens to the suits, the astronauts are in big trouble!"

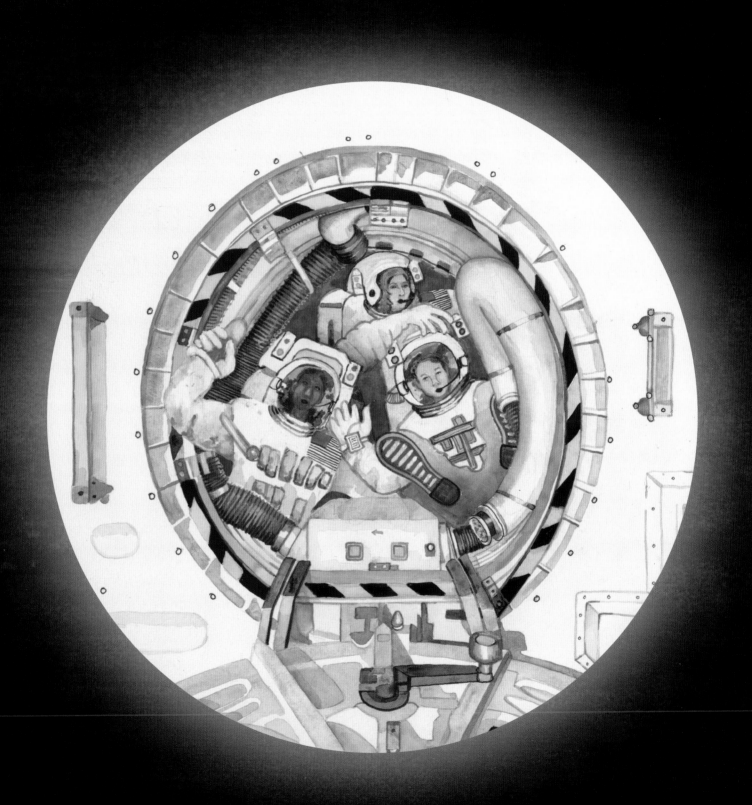

As one spacewalker struggles with the satellite, another astronaut seems to be in trouble. He twitches his face and scrunches his nose. He moans.

"What's wrong?" Ground Control asks anxiously. The astronaut moans again, and everyone waits for his answer.

"My nose is itchy, and I can't scratch it through the helmet!" We all breathe a sigh of relief.

Then the voice crackles over the radio again. "Houston, we have the satellite," Ground Control announces. "The mission is a success."

"Were you built just to rescue satellites?" I ask *Endeavour*.

"Oh, much more than that," she says. "I was built to replace the shuttle *Challenger*, who had an accident."

"We learned in school that one of the space shuttles actually blew up after it was launched," I say. "Was that *Challenger*?"

"Yes," says *Endeavour*. "After a small seal broke on one of the rockets during her launch, she never made it back home. The break caused the rocket to explode. Seven brave astronauts died on that mission. One of them was the very first teacher to go into space, Christa McAuliffe. She taught high school before she was trained to become an astronaut."

Endeavour explains in a brave voice, "The men and women who built *Challenger* were determined not to give up. With everyone's support behind them, they built me. I soared into space on my first mission in 1992."

"It must have been sad for everyone after what happened to your sister, but I'm glad that you were built." I smile. "Watching the satellite rescue is awesome."

As I float through the mid-deck, I see scientists busy working on various experiments

"I'd like you to meet my special team," *Endeavour* says.

"This young lady is Dr. Mae Jemison. I brought her into space, making her the first female African American astronaut. These young men are Dr. Mamoru Mohri, the first Japanese astronaut in the shuttle program, and John Herrington, the first Native American astronaut to walk in space."

"I didn't know astronauts were doctors!" I exclaim.

"Astronauts come from all walks of life. During my journeys, I brought doctors, engineers, pilots, astronomers, geologists, and many other types of astronauts into space," she explains.

"So there are different kinds of astronauts," I say.

"Yes, Jojo. Astronauts with different types of training and backgrounds work together as a team to complete many different types of projects."

This is getting more interesting. "Tell me about your other missions," I say.

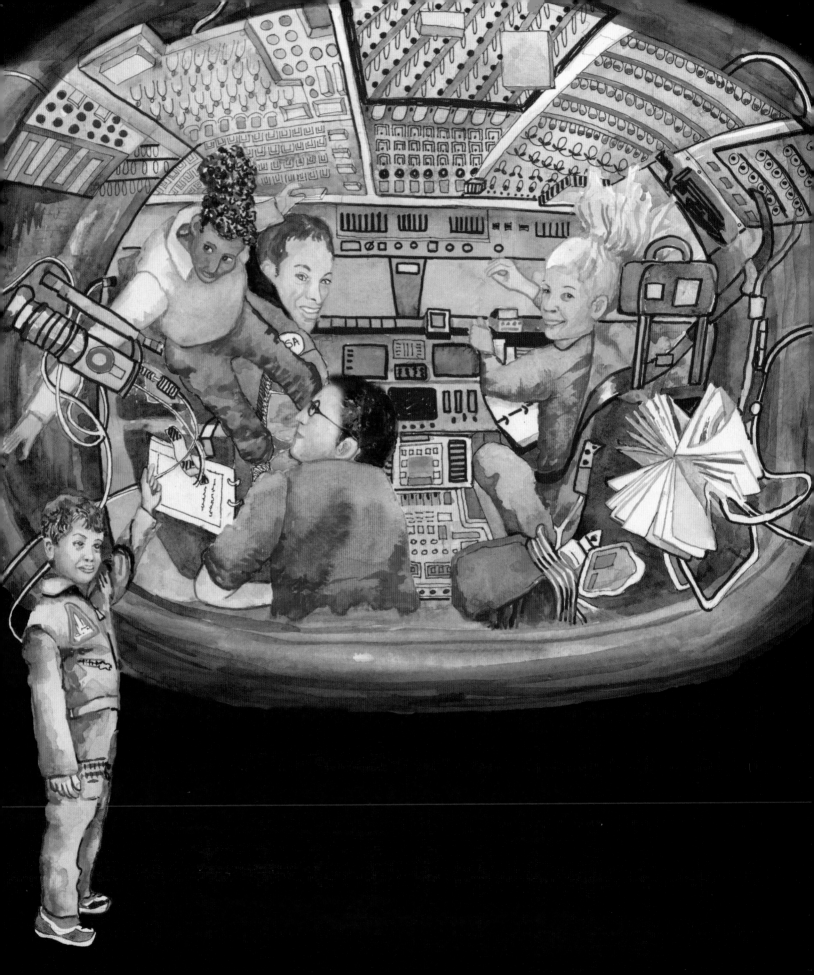

How can the Hubble Space Telescope see into the past?

It can take a long time for the light from stars to get to us. The sunlight we see every day takes about eight minutes to get here. So we see how the sun looked eight minutes earlier. Hubble can get clear images from billions of miles into space. When we see some distant stars, we see how they looked millions of years ago. Observing the most distant stars and galaxies, we can look far back in time, close to when the universe was formed. The universe is about 13.75 billion years old. How old is that? Well, modern humans have been on Earth only 200,000 years, which means that much of the light we see in the night sky actually left their stars well before humans ever even existed on our planet.

"In 1993, one of my most daring missions was to perform the very first eye operation in space," *Endeavour* says.

"Really! Who did you operate on?"

"It was an operation on the Hubble Space Telescope," she tells me. "It was a one-of-a-kind surgery to help Hubble see images deep into space, millions of miles away.

"What was wrong with the telescope?" I ask.

"Look outside my windows, and you'll see for yourself," *Endeavour* says. I watch as the astronauts catch the big telescope with a 50-foot robot arm and pull it into the shuttle's open payload bay.

"A few years earlier, the telescope was successfully launched into orbit, but its view became fuzzy because one of its mirrors was out of shape. So I brought a crew of astronauts to perform the very difficult task of fixing the fuzziness by putting 'glasses' on Hubble and adding new instruments," *Endeavour* explains.

The astronauts move so gently around the telescope in their bulky spacesuits. The crew inside are focused on their jobs, as are the spacewalkers. I can hear the concerned voices of the controllers back on Earth. The whole team works to fix the fragile telescope. Everything has to be done perfectly.

At last, the words the crew are waiting for come from Mission Control: "Great news, *Endeavour*! Your mission is complete. Hubble can see!" All the astronauts aboard *Endeavour* smile and hug each other in congratulations. The Hubble can now take the best pictures of the stars and galaxies ever taken. And the pictures are amazing.

"What other kind of missions were you on?" I ask excitedly.

"My final missions aimed to help build the International Space Station, also called ISS," *Endeavour* tells me. "I took the first crew to ever board the ISS, which at the time was a tiny space station, not much bigger than your school bus. Over 13 years, my sister shuttles and I took many trips there, slowly building it to the size it is today. The ISS now has people living in space permanently, and it is bigger than a football field, with more room inside than a large jet airplane."

"Wow, you sure have done a lot in space!"

I float through the flight deck of *Endeavour*.

"On June 1, 2011, I completed my last mission, journeying to the ISS one final time with an experiment to help scientists understand the beginnings of our universe," she continues. "You see, Jojo, my very long journey was not one that I took alone. Together with astronauts, scientists, engineers, and technicians, we explored space as a team of humans and the machines they made. In fact, it wouldn't surprise me if you know one of them."

Endeavour smiles mischievously.

I float to the back window. Looking off into the sky, deep in space, I see something that looks like two small clouds. "Clouds? But how can there be clouds in space?" I ask. "Space has no atmosphere."

"You are right. There are no clouds in space." she whispers back. "Look deeper, Jojo. What do you see?"

I look again and strain my eyes. Deeper and deeper I look. "Those are not clouds! They are filled with stars!"

"That's right. What you see are galaxies, groups of millions of stars," she explains. "They are called 'The Magellanic Clouds'—our two neighboring galaxies that are visible from Earth."

Distance to the Stars

The Sun is about 93 million miles away from Earth. The next nearest group of stars is Alpha Centauri. It is much further, trillions of miles away. So we measure the distance to stars in terms of light-years, which is how far light travels in a year. Light travels about 6 trillion miles in one year. Alpha Centauri is more than four light-years away. That basically means that the light from Alpha Centauri that we see today left it over four years ago. The furthest stars we have seen are billions of light-years away.

Millions and millions of stars, all clustered together, make what looks like the two hazy clouds. Here I am inside *Endeavour*, in my own Milky Way galaxy, looking at stars, far, far away. My mind begins to wonder: *Does that galaxy have a planet like Earth? Is there life there?* I wonder if something is there now, looking back at me, asking the same question.

"This is what's so special about space. For 19 years I flew, looking at sights like this," she says with pride. "After so many years of exploring, there are still many questions left unanswered."

As *Endeavour* tells me about the many questions she still has about the universe, I begin to float away from her. We drift further and further apart as I begin to fall back to Earth.

Then I hear that very familiar voice.

"JoJo," *Endeavour* whispers, "I've been on a long journey, and I'm happy I've been able to share my wonderful experience with you. I'm ready for a well-deserved rest. Go tell your friends to come visit me. I'll be here ready to take them on my incredible journey."

I am sad. I don't want the adventure to end. I want to fly with *Endeavour* and continue the exploration of space.

"Remember, I was built by people who believe that humans should explore space. Now it's your turn to dream and build the next ship to carry you and the next generation of astronauts to the great beyond.

"Dream your dreams, and make them happen. Explore all the secrets the universe has to share." Her voice becomes fainter...and then fades away.

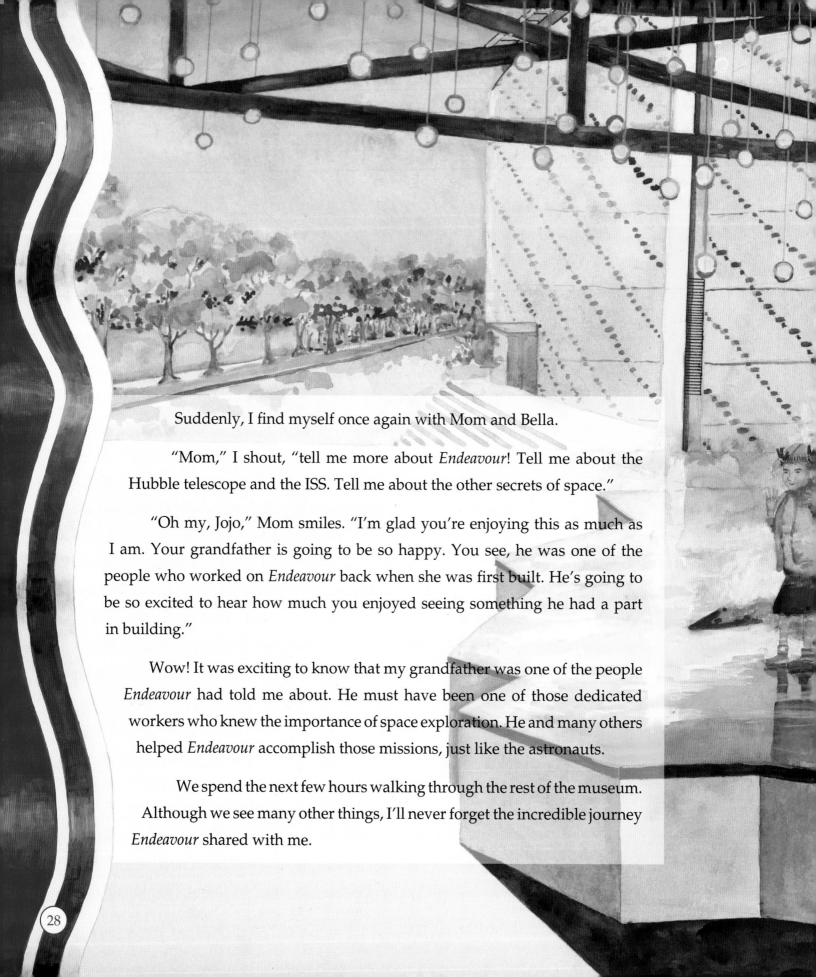

Suddenly, I find myself once again with Mom and Bella.

"Mom," I shout, "tell me more about *Endeavour*! Tell me about the Hubble telescope and the ISS. Tell me about the other secrets of space."

"Oh my, Jojo," Mom smiles. "I'm glad you're enjoying this as much as I am. Your grandfather is going to be so happy. You see, he was one of the people who worked on *Endeavour* back when she was first built. He's going to be so excited to hear how much you enjoyed seeing something he had a part in building."

Wow! It was exciting to know that my grandfather was one of the people *Endeavour* had told me about. He must have been one of those dedicated workers who knew the importance of space exploration. He and many others helped *Endeavour* accomplish those missions, just like the astronauts.

We spend the next few hours walking through the rest of the museum. Although we see many other things, I'll never forget the incredible journey *Endeavour* shared with me.

MEET *ENDEAVOUR*

Endeavour was the fifth and final spaceworthy shuttle built by the United States. It resides at the California Science Center in California. Her sisters *Atlantis* and *Discovery* presently reside at the Kennedy Space Center Visitor Complex in Florida and the Smithsonian's National Air and Space Museum in Washington DC, respectively. The very first orbiter, *Enterprise,* is at the Intrepid Sea, Air, and Space Museum in New York. Together with *Atlantis, Challenger, Columbia,* and *Discovery,* the shuttle fleet took astronauts from all over the world into space. They proved that humans could live and work in space. Together, they built a permanent colony in space, the International Space Station. Even today, astronauts live and work in a place that could never have existed had it not been for the men and women who comprised the space shuttle program.

ENDEAVOUR FUN FACTS

1

Named after an 18th-century ship led by Captain James Cook of Britain. The first and only shuttle named by elementary and secondary school students in a naming contest.

2

During *Endeavour*'s 25 missions, she traveled 123 million miles. That's about the same as 260 round trips from Earth to the Moon.

3

To reach its home at the California Science Center, *Endeavour* traveled 12 miles through the crowded streets of Inglewood and Los Angeles. The journey lasted 38 hours while about 1.5 million people filled the sidewalks to celebrate the historic event.

4

Endeavour was the youngest space shuttle. Her 19 years of flight missions ran from 1992 until she was retired in 2011.

5

The payload bay of *Endeavour* is big enough to carry cargo about the size of a school bus into and back from space.

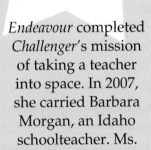

Endeavour completed *Challenger*'s mission of taking a teacher into space. In 2007, she carried Barbara Morgan, an Idaho schoolteacher. Ms. Morgan eventually became an astronaut.

7

The hottest part of the space shuttle's journey was during entry back into Earth's atmosphere—not launch! Returning home heated up the wings to about 3,000 degrees Fahrenheit or 1,650 degrees Celsius.

8

Two minutes after liftoff, when the rocket boosters fell away, the shuttle and external fuel tank were traveling at more than 3,000 miles per hour.

13

The waste generated by the fuel cells on *Endeavour* provided drinking water for the astronauts. These fuel cells also provided all electrical power to the spacecraft.

9

Endeavour is 122 feet long and 57 feet high, with a wingspan of 78 feet.

10

Endeavour was built from parts that remained from building *Discovery* and *Atlantis*.

11

The external fuel tank used on *Endeavour*'s last mission was damaged and repaired before launch, after being struck by Hurricane Katrina.

12

When fully loaded, *Endeavour* could carry as much as 54,000 pounds into space. That's about the same as carrying five full-grown elephants!

ENDEAVOUR'S FAMOUS FIRSTS

(Flight mission: 1992 – 2011)

MISSION POSSIBLE

Performed the first spacewalk involving three astronauts and four spacewalks— a risky maneuver!

Endeavour crewmembers of mission STS-49 hold onto a 4.5 ton satellite.

BREAKING BOUNDARIES

Carried the first African American female astronaut, Mae Jemison, into space; the first Japanese astronaut, Mamoru Mohri, in the shuttle program; and the first Native American astronaut, John Bennett Herrington of the Chickasaw Nation, to walk in space.

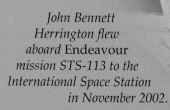

John Bennett Herrington flew aboard Endeavour mission STS-113 to the International Space Station in November 2002.

VISION QUEST

Completed the first service mission to the Hubble Space Telescope in 1993.

Astronaut F. Story Musgrave, anchored on the end of a robot arm, prepares to be lifted to the top of the Hubble Space Telescope for repair work.

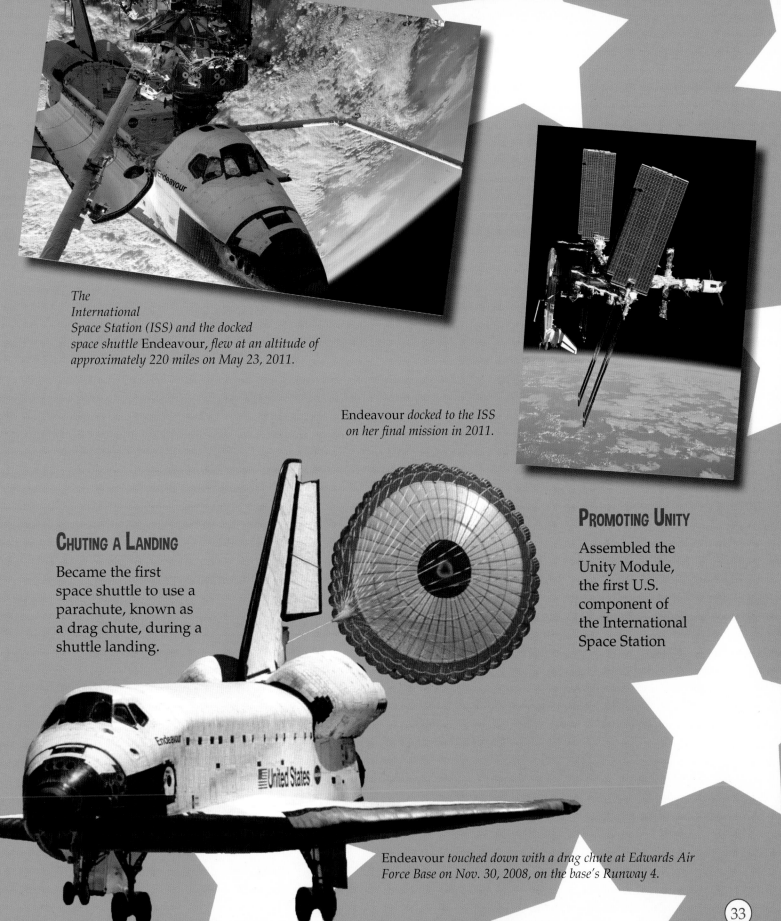

The International Space Station (ISS) and the docked space shuttle Endeavour, *flew at an altitude of approximately 220 miles on May 23, 2011.*

Endeavour *docked to the ISS on her final mission in 2011.*

CHUTING A LANDING

Became the first space shuttle to use a parachute, known as a drag chute, during a shuttle landing.

PROMOTING UNITY

Assembled the Unity Module, the first U.S. component of the International Space Station

Endeavour *touched down with a drag chute at Edwards Air Force Base on Nov. 30, 2008, on the base's Runway 4.*

Discovery's Famous Firsts

(Flight mission: 1984 – 2011)

- Holds the record of 39 flight missions, more than any other space shuttle or any spacecraft.

- Became the only shuttle ever to fly one of the original seven Mercury astronauts. John Glenn first flew in space in 1962, and then flew his second mission on *Discovery* in 1998—36 years later! John Glenn was not only the first American to orbit the Earth; he was also the oldest astronaut to fly in space at the age of 77.

- Carried American astronauts Eileen Collins, the first female to ever pilot a shuttle, and Bernard Harris, the first African American to walk in space, on the 1995 STS-63 mission, when *Discovery* linked up in orbit with Russia's Mir space station.

- Carried the first Russian cosmonaut, Sergei Krikalev, to launch in an American spacecraft, in 1994.

- Carried Ellen Ochoa, the first female Hispanic American to fly in space, aboard STS-56 in 1993.

- Deployed the Hubble Space Telescope in 1990.

Atlantis's Famous Firsts

(Flight mission: 1985 – 2011)

- Carried Rodolfo Neri Vela, the first Mexican in space, in 1985 on STS-61B.

- Carried Claude Nicollier, the first Swiss citizen to fly in space, aboard STS-46 in 1992.

- Became the first shuttle to dock with a space station, Mir, on STS-71 in 1995. It was also the 100th U.S.-manned space flight.

- Performed the final Hubble Space Telescope Servicing Mission 4 on STS-125 in 2009.

- Performed the final mission for the space shuttle program on STS-135 in 2011.

COLUMBIA'S FAMOUS FIRSTS

(Flight mission: 1981 – 2003)

- Became the very first space shuttle to fly in space.

- Completed the longest shuttle mission on STS-80 for a total of 17 days, 15 hours, and 53 minutes.

- Flew the smallest crew of only two astronauts on the very first shuttle mission of the space shuttle program.

- Became the first manned spacecraft to be reused, on November 12, 1981.

- Became the first spacecraft to carry a crew of six people into space and also flew the first Spacelab module in 1983.

- Carried Franklin Chang Diaz, the first Hispanic American in space, in 1986; the first Vietnamese American, Eugene Huu Chau Trinh, in 1992; and the first American female of Indian descent, Kalpana Chawla, in 1997.

- Became the only space shuttle to be destroyed during re-entry. On February 1, 2003, returning home, it disintegrated with all its crew members.

The Columbia *crew lost during STS-107 mission in 2003. Front row from left: astronauts Rick D. Husband, mission commander, and William C. McCool, pilot. Standing: astronauts David M. Brown, Laurel B. Clark, Kalpana Chawla and Michael P. Anderson, all mission specialists; and Ilan Ramon, payload specialist representing the Israeli Space Agency.*

CHALLENGER'S FAMOUS FIRSTS

(Flight mission: 1983 – 1986)

- Performed the first spacewalk during a space shuttle mission on April 4, 1983.

- Carried Dr. Sally Ride, the first American woman in space, in 1983. She was a mission specialist on STS-7.

- Carried Guion Stewart Bluford, the first African American in space, aboard STS-8 in 1983.

- Carried Kathryn D. Sullivan, the first American woman to make a spacewalk, in 1984. STS-41-G was the first mission to carry two women on the same mission, and also to carry Marc Garneau, the first Canadian in space.

- Carried Taylor Gun Jin Wang, the first ethnic Chinese person to go into space, in 1985.

- Lost seven crew members on the morning of Jan. 28, 1986, when a booster engine failed, causing the *Challenger* to break apart just 73 seconds after launch.

The lost Challenger *crew of STS-51-L: Front row from left: Mike Smith, Dick Scobee, Ron McNair. Back row: Ellison Onizuka, Christa McAuliffe, Greg Jarvis, Judith Resnik.*

SPACE QUIZ

1. Who was the first American astronaut to fly in space?

   a. Alan Shepard
   b. John Glenn
   c. Neil Armstrong
   d. Edwin Aldrin

2. Who was the first Hispanic American astronaut to fly in space?

   a. Fernando Caldeiro
   b. Franklin Chang-Diaz
   c. Ellen Ochoa
   d. John "Danny" Olivas

3. What makes up the main exhaust emitted by the space shuttle during launch?

   a. hydrogen
   b. carbon dioxide
   c. oxygen
   d. water

4. What country invented the first rockets?

   a. Soviet Union
   b. United States
   c. China
   d. Germany

5. How hot does the space shuttle get during re-entry to Earth's atmosphere from space?

   a. 30 degrees Farenheit
   b. 300 degrees Farenheit
   c. 900 degrees Farenheit
   d. 3,000 degrees Farenheit

6. How long does it take a space shuttle to go from 0 mph to over 17,000 mph during liftoff?

   a. 8 ½ minutes
   b. 30 minutes
   c. 2 hours
   d. 2 days

7. How much does an entire space shuttle weigh, including its tank and solid rocket motors?

   a. 2 million lbs.
   b. 6 million lbs.
   c. 8 million lbs.
   d. 10 million lbs.

8. Who was the only sitting U.S. President to personally witness a spacecraft launch?

   a. President Bill Clinton
   b. President John Kennedy
   c. President Ronald Reagan
   d. President Barack Obama

9. How long is a space shuttle?

   a. Three school buses long
   b. Five school buses long
   c. Seven school buses long
   d. Eight school buses long

10. Which was the only space shuttle never to fly in space?

    a. *Atlantis*
    b. *Challenger*
    c. *Columbia*
    d. *Enterprise*

Please see answers on page 38.

Endeavour's Final Journey to the California Science Center

The skyline of downtown Los Angeles pierces the mid-day haze above space shuttle Endeavour and its modified 747 Shuttle Carrier Aircraft during its flyover of Los Angeles landmarks near the conclusion of its Tour of California on its final ferry flight, Sept. 21, 2012.

Thousands of spectators gathered in front of the Forum in Inglewood, California, as Endeavour stopped temporarily for a celebration as it headed overland to its new home at the California Science Center in Los Angeles on Saturday, Oct. 13, 2012.

Endeavour is on display at the Samuel Oschin Space Shuttle Endeavour Display Pavilion at the California Science Center. Endeavour's ultimate mission is to inspire future generations of explorers and scientists.

GLOSSARY

air lock: a device that allows astronauts to go in and out of the spacecraft while in space

flight deck: where astronauts fly the space shuttle, similar to an airplane's cockpit

galaxy: a group of millions to trillions of stars, planets, and other materials held together by gravity

gravity: force of attraction between all objects in the universe

International Space Station (ISS): the permanent facility in space where astronauts from many countries conduct science and research

Magellanic Clouds: two galaxies neighboring our Milky Way galaxy that are visible from Earth without a telescope

meteorite: an object usually made of rock, which may originate from an asteroid or comet, that survives passage through the Earth's atmosphere and falls to Earth

mid-deck: the part of the space shuttle where astronauts eat, sleep, and work

Milky Way: galaxy that contains our Solar System and planet Earth

orbit: path followed by an object in space, such as a satellite or moon, as it travels around a larger object

payload bay: the "trunk" of the space shuttle, where large cargo is carried and astronauts can spacewalk to build and fix spacecraft

satellite: object that travels in orbit around another object, such as the Moon traveling around Earth

shuttle: a reusable spacecraft to take and return items and people from space

spacewalk: an astronaut's venture outside the spacecraft to perform a mission in space

ONLINE RESOURCES

www.nasa.gov/education

The NASA Office of Education provides informative educational materials on the Space Shuttle Program, Space Exploration, and educational activities for students K-12.

www.airandspace.si.edu/exhibitions

The National Air and Space Museum features a wide variety of online and on-view exhibits on the history of space exploration.

http://amazing-space.stsci.edu

This site contains activities that use the Hubble Space Telescope's discoveries to inspire and educate about the wonders of our universe.

Quiz Answers: 1.a 2.b 3.d 4.c 5.d 6.a 7.c 8.a 9.a 10.d

About the Author

John "Danny" Olivas, PhD, PE, born in North Hollywood, is a former NASA astronaut. Dr. Olivas has traveled more than 11.6 million miles in space, on two U.S. Space Shuttle missions, STS-117 on Atlantis and STS-128 on *Discovery*, to the International Space Station. His other NASA missions include living at the bottom of the ocean in an underwater habitat, surviving the frozen Arctic, trekking across the mountains of Wyoming, and sailing the sea of Cortez.

Dr. Olivas retired from NASA in 2010 and now resides in the Los Angeles area with his wife and five children. He has shared his space stories with children here at home as well as internationally. Now he shares one of his stories in his first book. Olivas's motto of "Dream Big Dreams" is one he wishes to pass onto the next generation of explorers.

About the Illustrator

Gayle Garner Roski is the award-winning illustrator of *Mei Ling in China City* and for *Thomas the T. rex*, which has been selected as the 2012 Outstanding Science Trade Books for Students K-12, the Book of the Year Award for the Educational Storybook by Creative Child Magazine, and a Gold Medal winner of the Mom's Choice Award in the Juvenile Historical Fiction category.

A celebrated watercolorist, Mrs. Roski is the Commissioner of Cultural Affairs for the city of Los Angeles, Chairman of the Art Committee for the Los Angeles Cathedral, and a Board Member of the University of Southern California Fine Arts Department, which bears her name.

About the Editors

Icy Smith is the author and editor of many acclaimed historical fiction and nonfiction books. She is the recipient of numerous prestigious book awards including the National Joint Conference of Librarians of Color Author Award for her contributions to the understanding of diversity and history in the United States and the world. Her newest title, *Three Years and Eight Months*, documents the hardships and human endurance of ordinary people in Hong Kong during the Japanese occupation in World War II.

Michael Smith is the author of numerous nonfiction and fiction books. Among his many award-winning titles are *What in the World!*, *World Trivia*, *Relativity*, a Junior Library Guild Selection, and *Thomas the T. rex*, an Outstanding Science Trade Book for K-12.

Mama scolded and then she purred:
"Never should a kitty try to be a bird."

All the kitties hugged their brother,
Then, shame-faced, listened to their mother.

And quickly rescued her littlest baby.

"Tsking-tsking," she climbed the tree

And every kitty ran to hide.

Mama Cat rushed outside

And the mountain of kitties crumbled;
Down to the ground they all tumbled.

But suddenly, a springtime breeze
Made the kitties start to sneeze!

Holding a bright blue parasol,
Climbed up higher than all the others,
And reached the top branch of the tree....

Making a mountain next to the tree,
That reached up high as high could be.
Then the teensiest one of all,

"Let's make a mountain," the kitties giggled.
So every kitty climbed and wiggled.

They hadn't feathers; they hadn't wings.
Kitties do not have such things.

The kitties cried, "Oh, let's fly, too!"
But how to fly, no one knew!

A mother robin, way up high,
Was teaching her babies how to fly.

One bright and sunny springtime day,

ITSY-BITSIES Storybooks™

Kitties'
Purr-fect Caper

Written by Gary Poole
Illustrated by Kathleen Smith-Fitzpatrick

MODERN PUBLISHING
A Division of Unisystems, Inc.
New York, New York 10022

Table of Contents

★ Introduction ★

Team-Teaching Interdisciplinary Strategies and Activities integrates American history and American literature, an approach often referred to as "humanities." The purpose of *Team-Teaching Interdisciplinary Strategies and Activities* is to contribute to the creation of an environment that leads to meaningful student learning. As students face increasingly rigorous academic standards and testing, teachers continue to search for effective means to reinforce student learning. Team-teaching history and literature is an instructional approach that allows students to construct the "whole picture" of a historical period, leading to meaningful learning.

Team-Teaching Interdisciplinary Strategies and Activities for *The American Vision* was designed primarily to address two teaching constructs: the history–literature aspect of a humanities team and the history teacher who is integrating literature into the history curriculum. Generally, a team-teaching construct is comprised of two to four content teachers who integrate their respective curriculums for presentation to a core group of students.

Each page in this booklet includes background information about an historical event or period as discussed in *The American Vision*. This background information is accompanied by a synopsis of a piece of literature in Glencoe's *The*

Reader's Choice: American Literature. The chronological orientation of both Glencoe's history and literature texts contributes to meaningful integration. For teachers who may not have access to Glencoe's literature series, the literary selections included in this booklet are easily obtainable from a library or the Internet.

Team-Teaching Interdisciplinary Strategies and Activities supports the history teacher who wishes to reinforce historical concepts through a literary interface. Each strategy presents sufficient information to build a literary connection, even if literature is not the content area of expertise for the instructor. Each piece of literature is discussed, and excerpts are included to support discussion points. Each strategy also includes questions for discussion and writing prompts. Where applicable, the activities integrate both the historical and literary components of the lesson; however, some activities emphasize the literary connection.

Upon students' completion of an activity, the team-teachers may choose to share evaluation duties. This may require the teachers to develop rubrics to ensure consistent evaluation. Other teams may choose one teacher to evaluate content, while another instructor evaluates structure and composition.

Additional Literature Selections and Activities

The 34 suggested literature pieces presented in this booklet will initiate integration of the history–language arts curriculums, but numerous additional connections between literature and history can be developed. On pages vii–xvi of this booklet, you will find unit correlations of five course textbooks from Glencoe's Literature series, *The Reader's Choice,* to *The American Vision.* The correlations suggest many titles from a variety of genres. The correlations also provide links to Web sites that offer activities and additional information about the selections and authors.

The key below explains how to utilize the correlation charts:

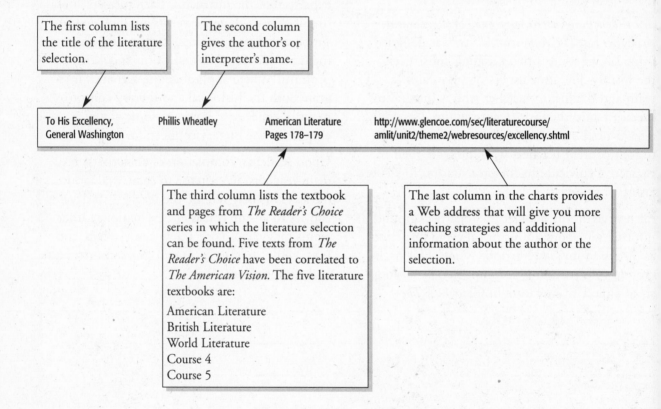

The first column lists the title of the literature selection.

The second column gives the author's or interpreter's name.

| To His Excellency, General Washington | Phillis Wheatley | American Literature Pages 178–179 | http://www.glencoe.com/sec/literaturecourse/ amlit/unit2/theme2/webresources/excellency.shtml |

The third column lists the textbook and pages from *The Reader's Choice* series in which the literature selection can be found. Five texts from *The Reader's Choice* have been correlated to *The American Vision.* The five literature textbooks are:

American Literature
British Literature
World Literature
Course 4
Course 5

The last column in the charts provides a Web address that will give you more teaching strategies and additional information about the author or the selection.

Unit 1: Three Worlds Meet, Beginnings–1763

Selection Title	Author	The Reader's Choice Text & Location	Web Link
Anansi's Fishing Expedition	translated by Harold Courlander and George Herzog	World Literature Pages 59–62	http://www.glencoe.com/sec/literature/course/wrldlit/unit1/part1/webresources/anansi.shtml
from The Annals: The Burning of Rome	Tacitus	World Literature Pages 393–396	http://www.glencoe.com/sec/literature/course/wrldlit/unit2/part2/webresources/rome.shtml
from the Apology from the Dialogues	Plato	World Literature Pages 328–331	http://www.glencoe.com/sec/literature/course/wrldlit/unit2/part1/webresources/apology.shtml
Coyote Finishes His Work	retold by Barry Lopez	World Literature Pages 1048–1049	http://www.glencoe.com/sec/literature/course/wrldlit/unit6/part1/webresources/coyote.shtml
from the Decameron: Federigo's Falcon	Giovanni Boccaccio	World Literature Pages 829–833	http://www.glencoe.com/sec/literature/course/wrldlit/unit5/part1/webresources/decameron.shtml
from A Dictionary of the English Language	Samuel Johnson	British Literature Pages 609–612	http://www.glencoe.com/sec/literature/course/brlit/unit3/theme6/webresources/dictionary.shtml
Discoveries	Eduardo Langagne	World Literature Page 1068	http://www.glencoe.com/sec/literature/course/wrldlit/unit6/part1/webresources/discoveries.shtml
The Dog and the Wolf	Aesop	World Literature Page 251	http://www.glencoe.com/sec/literature/course/wrldlit/unit2/part1/webresources/dogandwolf.shtml
from Don Quixote	Miguel de Cervantes	World Literature Pages 837–843	http://www.glencoe.com/sec/literature/course/wrldlit/unit5/part1/webresources/quixote.shtml
Edju and the Two Friends	translated by Paul Radin	World Literature Pages 65–66	http://www.glencoe.com/sec/literature/course/wrldlit/unit1/part1/webresources/edju.shtml
Eldorado	Edgar Allan Poe	Course 5 Page 583	http://www.glencoe.com/sec/literature/course/course5/unit3/theme7/webresources/active.shtml
from The Histories	Herodotus	American Literature Pages 161–165	http://www.glencoe.com/sec/literature/course/amlit/unit2/theme2/webresources/histories.shtml
How the World Was Made	retold by James Mooney	American Literature Pages 48–49	http://www.glencoe.com/sec/literature/course/amlit/unit1/theme1/webresources/howtheworld.shtml
from the Iliad	Homer	World Literature Pages 213–244	http://www.glencoe.com/sec/literature/course/wrldlit/unit2/part1/webresources/iliad.shtml
from The Iroquois Constitution	Dekanawida	American Literature Pages 55–57	http://www.glencoe.com/sec/literature/course/amlit/unit1/theme1/webresources/iroquois.shtml
from A Journal of the Plague Year	Daniel Defoe	British Literature Pages 590–593	http://www.glencoe.com/sec/literature/course/brlit/unit3/theme6/webresources/plague.shtml
from La Relación	Álvar Núñez Cabeza de Vaca	American Literature Pages 62–65	http://www.glencoe.com/sec/literature/course/amlit/unit1/theme1/webresources/larelacion.shtml
from The Life of Olaudah Equiano	Olaudah Equiano	American Literature Pages 189–194	http://www.glencoe.com/sec/literature/course/amlit/unit2/theme2/webresources/thelife.shtml
from Of Plymouth Plantation	William Bradford	American Literature Pages 69–72	http://www.glencoe.com/sec/literature/course/amlit/unit1/theme1/webresources/plymouth.shtml
On Monsieur's Departure	Elizabeth I	British Literature Page 251	http://www.glencoe.com/sec/literature/course/brlit/unit2/theme2/webresources/monsieur.shtml
The Tragedy of Julius Caesar	William Shakespeare	Course 5 Pages 778–870	http://www.glencoe.com/sec/literature/course/course5/unit4/theme10/webresources/caesar.shtml
Upon the Burning of Our House	Anne Bradstreet	American Literature Pages 77–78	http://www.glencoe.com/sec/literature/course/amlit/unit1/theme1/webresources/uponburning.shtml
from The Voyage of Christopher Columbus	Christopher Columbus	World Literature Pages 1059–1064	http://www.glencoe.com/sec/literature/course/wrldlit/unit6/part1/webresources/columbus.shtml

Unit 2: Creating a Nation, 1754–1816

Selection Title	Author	The Reader's Choice Text & Location	Web Link
from The Autobiography of Benjamin Franklin	Benjamin Franklin	American Literature Pages 131–133	http://www.glencoe.com/sec/literature/course/amlit/unit2/theme2/webresources/franklin.shtml
from Poor Richard's Almanack	Benjamin Franklin	American Literature Pages 134–135	http://www.glencoe.com/sec/literature/course/amlit/unit2/theme2/webresources/almanac.shtml
Declaration of Independence	Thomas Jefferson	American Literature Pages 169–172	http://www.glencoe.com/sec/literature/course/amlit/unit2/theme2/webresources/independence.shtml
from The Crisis, No. 1	Thomas Paine	American Literature Pages 155–157	http://www.glencoe.com/sec/literature/course/amlit/unit2/theme2/webresources/crisis.shtml
Let Us Examine the Facts	Corn Tassel	American Literature Pages 519–520	http://www.glencoe.com/sec/literature/course/amlit/unit4/theme6/webresources/letusexamine.shtml
Letter to Her Daughter from the New and Unfinished White House	Abigail Adams	American Literature Pages 183–185	http://www.glencoe.com/sec/literature/course/amlit/unit2/theme2/webresources/whitehouse.shtml
Old Ironsides	Oliver Wendell Holmes	American Literature Page 225	http://www.glencoe.com/sec/literature/course/amlit/unit2/theme3/webresources/ironsides.shtml
Speech to the Second Virginia Convention	Patrick Henry	American Literature Pages 147–149	http://www.glencoe.com/sec/literature/course/amlit/unit2/theme2/webresources/virginia.shtml
Thanatopsis	William Cullen Bryant	American Literature Pages 220–222	http://www.glencoe.com/sec/literature/course/amlit/unit2/theme3/webresources/waterfowl.shtml
To a Waterfowl	William Cullen Bryant	American Literature Page 219	http://www.glencoe.com/sec/literature/course/amlit/unit2/theme3/webresources/waterfowl.shtml
To His Excellency, General Washington	Phillis Wheatley	American Literature Pages 178–179	http://www.glencoe.com/sec/literature/course/amlit/unit2/theme2/webresources/excellency.shtml

Unit 3: The Young Republic, 1789–1850

Selection Title	Author	The Reader's Choice Text & Location	Web Link
from Big River: The Adventures of Huckleberry Finn	William Hauptman	Course 5 Pages 717–719	http://www.glencoe.com/sec/literature/course/course5/unit4/theme10/webresources/active.shtml
from Civil Disobedience	Henry David Thoreau	American Literature Pages 257–261	http://www.glencoe.com/sec/literature/course/amlit/unit2/theme3/webresources/walden.shtml
The First Snow-Fall	James Russell Lowell	American Literature Pages 231–232	http://www.glencoe.com/sec/literature/course/amlit/unit2/theme3/webresources/firstsnow.shtml
Lineage	Margaret Walker	Course 4 Page 546	http://www.glencoe.com/sec/literature/course/course4/unit3/theme8/webresources/lineage.shtml
from Songs of Gold Mountain	Anonymous	American Literature Pages 675–676	http://www.glencoe.com/sec/literature/course/amlit/unit5/theme7/webresources/mountain.shtml
The Tide Rises, the Tide Falls	Henry Wadsworth Longfellow	American Literature Page 236	http://www.glencoe.com/sec/literature/course/amlit/unit2/theme3/webresources/risefall.shtml
from Walden	Henry David Thoreau	American Literature Pages 252–255	http://www.glencoe.com/sec/literature/course/amlit/unit2/theme3/webresources/walden.shtml
Where Are Those Songs?	Micere Githae Mugo	Course 4 Pages 547–548	http://www.glencoe.com/sec/literature/course/course4/unit3/theme8/webresources/lineage.shtml
The Devil and Tom Walker	Washington Irving	American Literature Pages 203–213	http://www.glencoe.com/sec/literature/course/amlit/unit2/theme3/webresources/devil.shtml
The Outcasts of Poker Flat	Bret Harte	American Literature Pages 476–484	http://www.glencoe.com/sec/literature/course/amlit/unit4/theme6/webresources/outcasts.shtml

Unit 4: The Crisis of Union, 1848–1877

Selection Title	Author	The Reader's Choice Text & Location	Web Link
And Ain't I a Woman?	Sojourner Truth	American Literature Pages 345–346	http://www.glencoe.com/sec/literature/course/amlit/unit3/theme4/webresources/aint.shtml
Beat! Beat! Drums!	Walt Whitman	American Literature Page 407	http://www.glencoe.com/sec/literature/course/amlit/unit3/theme5/webresources/sight.shtml
Douglass	Paul Laurence Dunbar	American Literature Page 543	http://www.glencoe.com/sec/literature/course/amlit/unit4/theme6/webresources/douglass.shtml
Follow the Drinking Gourd	Anonymous	American Literature Page 339	http://www.glencoe.com/sec/literature/course/amlit/unit3/theme4/webresources/swinglow.shtml
The Gettysburg Address	Abraham Lincoln	American Literature Page 385	http://www.glencoe.com/sec/literature/course/amlit/unit3/theme4/webresources/address.shtml
Go Down, Moses	Anonymous	American Literature Page 338	http://www.glencoe.com/sec/literature/course/amlit/unit3/theme4/webresources/swinglow.shtml
from His Promised Land	John P. Parker	American Literature Pages 350–352	http://www.glencoe.com/sec/literature/course/amlit/unit3/theme4/webresources/promisedland.shtml
I Hear America Singing	Walt Whitman	American Literature Page 403	http://www.glencoe.com/sec/literature/course/amlit/unit3/theme5/webresources/singing.shtml
Letters to His Family	Robert E. Lee	American Literature Pages 363–364	http://www.glencoe.com/sec/literature/course/amlit/unit3/theme4/webresources/letters.shtml
from Mary Chesnut's Civil War	Mary Chesnut	American Literature Pages 357–360	http://www.glencoe.com/sec/literature/course/amlit/unit3/theme4/webresources/civilwar.shtml
from My Bondage and My Freedom	Frederick Douglass	American Literature Pages 330–334	http://www.glencoe.com/sec/literature/course/amlit/unit3/theme4/webresources/bondage.shtml
An Occurrence at Owl Creek Bridge	Ambrose Bierce	American Literature Pages 368–376	http://www.glencoe.com/sec/literature/course/amlit/unit3/theme4/webresources/owlcreek.shtml
Shiloh	Herman Melville	American Literature Page 382	http://www.glencoe.com/sec/literature/course/amlit/unit3/theme4/webresources/shiloh.shtml
A Sight in Camp in the Daybreak Gray and Dim	Walt Whitman	American Literature Page 406	http://www.glencoe.com/sec/literature/course/amlit/unit3/theme5/webresources/sight.shtml
Swing Low, Sweet Chariot	Anonymous	American Literature Page 337	http://www.glencoe.com/sec/literature/course/amlit/unit3/theme4/webresources/swinglow.shtml
We Wear the Mask	Paul Laurence Dunbar	American Literature Page 544	http://www.glencoe.com/sec/literature/course/amlit/unit4/theme6/webresources/douglass.shtml

Unit 5: The Birth of Modern America, 1865–1900

Selection Title	Author	The Reader's Choice Text & Location	Web Link
Before the End of Summer	Grant Moss Jr.	Course 4 Pages 25–37	http://www.glencoe.com/sec/literature/course/course4/unit1/theme1/webresources/beforeend.shtml
The Californian's Tale	Mark Twain	Course 5 Pages 248–254	http://www.glencoe.com/sec/literature/course/course5/unit1/theme3/webresources/californian.shtml
The Gift of the Magi	O. Henry	Course 4 Pages 7–13	http://www.glencoe.com/sec/literature/course/course4/unit1/theme1/webresources/magi.shtml
Heaven	Cathy Song	Course 5 Pages 624–625	http://www.glencoe.com/sec/literature/course/course5/unit3/theme8/webresources/fragment.shtml
I Will Fight No More Forever	Chief Joseph	American Literature Page 514	http://www.glencoe.com/sec/literature/course/amlit/unit4/theme6/webresources/fightnomore.shtml
from Life on the Mississippi	Mark Twain	Course 4 Pages 285–290	http://www.glencoe.com/sec/literature/course/course4/unit2/theme4/webresources/mississippi.shtml
The Love Song of J. Alfred Prufrock	T. S. Eliot	American Literature Pages 604–608	http://www.glencoe.com/sec/literature/course/amlit/unit5/theme7/webresources/love.shtml
The Open Boat	Stephen Crane	American Literature Pages 559–575	http://www.glencoe.com/sec/literature/course/amlit/unit4/theme6/webresources/openboat.shtml
The Story of an Hour	Kate Chopin	American Literature Pages 525–527	http://www.glencoe.com/sec/literature/course/amlit/unit4/theme6/webresources/storyofanhour.shtml
To Build a Fire	Jack London	American Literature Pages 498–509	http://www.glencoe.com/sec/literature/course/amlit/unit4/theme6/webresources/tobuild.shtml
The United States vs. Susan B. Anthony	Margaret Truman	Course 4 Pages 354–364	http://www.glencoe.com/sec/literature/course/course4/unit2/theme5/webresources/theus.shtml
A Wagner Matinée	Willa Cather	American Literature Pages 532–539	http://www.glencoe.com/sec/literature/course/amlit/unit4/theme6/webresources/wagner.shtml
Where the Girl Rescued Her Brother	Joseph Bruchac and Gayle Ross	Course 5 Pages 983–986	http://www.glencoe.com/sec/literature/course/course5/unit5/theme11/webresources/rescued.shtml

Unit 6: Imperialism and Progressivism, 1890–1919

Selection Title	Author	The Reader's Choice Text & Location	Web Link
Dreamers	Siegfried Sassoon	British Literature Page 1005	http://www.glencoe.com/sec/literature/course/ brlit/unit6/theme11/webresources/soldier.shtml
Dulce et Decorum est	Wilfred Owen	British Literature Page 1004	http://www.glencoe.com/sec/literature/course/ brlit/unit6/theme11/webresources/soldier.shtml
If We Must Die	Claude McKay	American Literature Page 734	http://www.glencoe.com/sec/literature/course/ amlit/unit5/theme8/webresources/mustdie.shtml
In Another Country	Ernest Hemingway	American Literature Pages 680–683	http://www.glencoe.com/sec/literature/course/ amlit/unit5/theme7/webresources/country.shtml
An Irish Airman Foresees His Death	William Butler Yeats	British Literature Page 1029	http://www.glencoe.com/sec/literature/course/ brlit/unit6/theme11/webresources/innisfree.shtml
Kipling and I	Jesus Colon	Course 4 Pages 319–321	http://www.glencoe.com/sec/literature/course/ course4/unit2/theme4/webresources/kipling.shtml
The Scarlet Ibis	James Hurst	Course 4 Pages 257–267	http://www.glencoe.com/sec/literature/course/ course4/unit1/theme3/webresources/scarlet.shtml
The Second Coming	William Butler Yeats	British Literature Page 1030	http://www.glencoe.com/sec/literature/course/ brlit/unit6/theme11/webresources/innisfree.shtml
The Soldier	Rupert Brooke	British Literature Page 1003	http://www.glencoe.com/sec/literature/course/ brlit/unit6/theme11/webresources/soldier.shtml
The Window	Jaime Torres Bodet	World Literature Page 1103	http://www.glencoe.com/sec/literature/course/ wrldlit/unit6/part2/webresources/window.shtml

Unit 7: Boom and Bust, 1920–1941

Selection Title	Author	The Reader's Choice Text & Location	Web Link
Afro-American Fragment	Langston Hughes	Course 5 Page 623	http://www.glencoe.com/sec/literature/course/course5/unit3/theme8/webresources/fragment.shtml
Any Human to Another	Countee Cullen	American Literature Page 759	http://www.glencoe.com/sec/literature/course/amlit/unit5/theme8/webresources/reaping.shtml
A black man talks of reaping	Arna Bontemps	American Literature Page 758	http://www.glencoe.com/sec/literature/course/amlit/unit5/theme8/webresources/reaping.shtml
from Black Boy	Richard Wright	Course 4 Pages 297–300	http://www.glencoe.com/sec/literature/course/course4/unit2/theme4/webresources/fromblack.shtml
Breakfast	John Steinbeck	American Literature Pages 798–800	http://www.glencoe.com/sec/literature/course/amlit/unit6/theme9/webresources/breakfast.shtml
The Bridal Party	F. Scott Fitzgerald	American Literature Pages 652–665	http://www.glencoe.com/sec/literature/course/amlit/unit5/theme7/webresources/bridal.shtml
The Car We Had to Push	James Thurber	Course 5 Pages 1045–1049	http://www.glencoe.com/sec/literature/course/course5/unit6/theme12/webresources/thecar.shtml
Chicago	Carl Sandburg	American Literature Pages 671–672	http://www.glencoe.com/sec/literature/course/amlit/unit5/theme7/webresources/chicago.shtml
A Christmas Memory	Truman Capote	Course 4 Pages 405–416	http://www.glencoe.com/sec/literature/course/course4/unit2/theme5/webresources/christmas.shtml
Ex-Basketball Player	John Updike	Course 5 Pages 636–637	http://www.glencoe.com/sec/literature/course/course5/unit3/theme8/webresources/player.shtml
The Glory of the Day was in Her Face	James Weldon Johnson	Course 5 Page 597	http://www.glencoe.com/sec/literature/course/course5/unit3/theme7/webresources/glory.shtml
I, Too	Langston Hughes	American Literature Page 740	http://www.glencoe.com/sec/literature/course/amlit/unit5/theme8/webresources/itoo.shtml
Jazz Fantasia	Carl Sandburg	Course 5 Pages 699	http://www.glencoe.com/sec/literature/course/course5/unit3/theme9/webresources/spirit.shtml
The Life You Save May Be Your Own	Flannery O'Connor	American Literature Pages 7–17	http://www.glencoe.com/sec/literature/course/amlit/unit1/theme1/webresources/arm_life.shtml
Mrs. James	Alice Childress	Course 5 Page 305	http://www.glencoe.com/sec/literature/course/course5/unit1/theme3/webresources/mrsjames.shtml
My City	James Weldon Johnson	American Literature Page 720	http://www.glencoe.com/sec/literature/course/amlit/unit5/theme8/webresources/mycity.shtml
Of Dry Goods and Black Bow Ties	Yoshiko Uchida	Course 4 Pages 395–399	http://www.glencoe.com/sec/literature/course/course4/unit2/theme5/webresources/drygoods.shtml
Sonnet to a Negro in Harlem	Helene Johnson	American Literature Page 749	http://www.glencoe.com/sec/literature/course/amlit/unit5/theme8/webresources/harlem.shtml
The Tropics in New York	Claude McKay	American Literature Page 735	http://www.glencoe.com/sec/literature/course/amlit/unit5/theme8/webresources/mustdie.shtml
A Worn Path	Eudora Welty	American Literature Pages 833–839	http://www.glencoe.com/sec/literature/course/amlit/unit6/theme9/webresources/wornpath.shtml

Unit 8: Global Struggles, 1934–1960

Selection Title	Author	The Reader's Choice Text & Location	Web Link
The Bass, the River, and Sheila Mant	W. D. Wetherell	Course 4 Pages 199–205	http://www.glencoe.com/sec/literature/course/course4/unit1/theme3/webresources/thebass.shtml
Be Ye Men of Valor	Winston Churchill	British Literature Pages 1113–1116	http://www.glencoe.com/sec/literature/course/brlit/unit6/theme11/webresources/valor.shtml
Blues Ain't No Mockin Bird	Toni Cade Bambara	Course 4 Pages 98–103	http://www.glencoe.com/sec/literature/course/course4/unit1/theme1/webresources/blues.shtml
The Crucible	Arthur Miller	American Literature Pages 913–995	http://www.glencoe.com/sec/literature/course//amlit/unit6/theme10webresources/crucible.shtml
The Death of the Ball Turret Gunner	Randall Jarrell	American Literature Page 857	http://www.glencoe.com/sec/literature/course/amlit/unit6/theme9/webresources/death.shtml
The Demon Lover	Elizabeth Bowen	British Literature Pages 1119–1125	http://www.glencoe.com/sec/literature/course/brlit/unit6/theme11/webresources/lover.shtml
from Farewell to Manzanar	Jeanne Wakatsuki Houston and James D. Houston	Course 5 Pages 460–471	http://www.glencoe.com/sec/literature/course/course5/unit2/theme5/webresources/manzanar.shtml
How I Changed the War and Won the Game	Mary Helen Ponce	Course 5 Pages 1055–1056	http://www.glencoe.com/sec/literature/course/course5/unit6/theme12/webresources/changed.shtml
from Kubota	Garrett Hongo	American Literature Pages 1101–1106	http://www.glencoe.com/sec/literature/course/amlit/unit7/theme11/webresources/kubota.shtml
The Leap	Louise Erdrich	Course 4 Pages 57–63	http://www.glencoe.com/sec/literature/course/course4/unit1/theme1/webresources/theleap.shtml
Living Well. Living Good.	Maya Angelou	Course 5 Pages 489–491	http://www.glencoe.com/sec/literature/course/course5/unit2/theme5/webresources/living.shtml
Naming of Parts	Henry Reed	British Literature Page 1152	http://www.glencoe.com/sec/literature/course/brlit/unit6/theme12/webresources/expected.shtml
from Night	Elie Wiesel	World Literature Pages 1001–1005	http://www.glencoe.com/sec/literature/course/wrldlit/unit5/part2/webresources/fromnight.shtml
Pizza in Warsaw, Torte in Prague	Slavenka Drakulic	Course 5 Pages 507–512	http://www.glencoe.com/sec/literature/course/course5/unit2/theme6/webresources/pizza.shtml
The Portrait	Tomás Rivera	American Literature Pages 851–853	http://www.glencoe.com/sec/literature/course/amlit/unit6/theme9/webresources/portrait.shtml
Rules of the Game	Amy Tan	Course 4 Pages 225–233	http://www.glencoe.com/sec/literature/course/course4/unit1/theme3/webresources/rules.shtml
The Secret Life of Walter Mitty	James Thurber	Course 4 Pages 116–120	http://www.glencoe.com/sec/literature/course/course4/unit1/theme2/webresources/mitty.shtml
Snow	Julia Alvarez	American Literature Page 1032	http://www.glencoe.com/sec/literature/course/amlit/unit7/theme11/webresources/snow.shtml
Soldiers of the Republic	Dorothy Parker	American Literature Pages 689–691	http://www.glencoe.com/sec/literature/course/amlit/unit5/theme7/webresources/soldiers.shtml
Sweet Potatoe Pie	Eugenia Collier	Course 4 Pages 212–219	http://www.glencoe.com/sec/literature/course/course4/unit1/theme3/webresources/sweetpotato.shtml
Two Kinds	Amy Tan	Course 5 Pages 49–58	http://www.glencoe.com/sec/literature/course/course5/unit1/theme1/webresources/twokinds.shtml
What I Expected	Stephen Spender	British Literature Page 1150	http://www.glencoe.com/sec/literature/course/brlit/unit6/theme12/webresources/expected.shtml
Winter Night	Kay Boyle	Course 5 Pages 363–371	http://www.glencoe.com/sec/literature/course/course5/unit1/theme4/webresources/winternight.shtml

Unit 9: A Time of Upheaval, 1954–1980

Selection Title	Author	The Reader's Choice Text & Location	Web Link
Ambush	Tim O'Brien	American Literature Pages 1063–1064	http://www.glencoe.com/sec/literature/course/amlit/unit7/theme11/webresources/ambush.shtml
from An American Childhood	Annie Dillard	Course 5 Pages 1030–1035	http://www.glencoe.com/sec/literature/course/course5/unit6/theme12/webresources/childhood.shtml
American History	Judith Ortiz Cofer	Course 4 Pages 156–162	http://www.glencoe.com/sec/literature/course/course4/unit1/theme2/webresources/americanhistory.shtml
And Sarah Laughed	Joanne Greenberg	Course 4 Pages 135–146	http://www.glencoe.com/sec/literature/course/course4/unit1/theme2/webresources/sarah.shtml
Assembly Line	Shu Ting	World Literature Page 674	http://www.glencoe.com/sec/literature/course/wrldlit/unit4/part1/webresources/assembly.shtml
Chee's Daughter	Juanita Platero and Siyowin Miller	Course 5 Pages 23–34	http://www.glencoe.com/sec/literature/course/course5/unit1/theme1/webresources/chees.shtml
Choice: A Tribute to Dr. Martin Luther King, Jr.	Alice Walker	American Literature Pages 898–900	http://www.glencoe.com/sec/literature/course/amlit/unit6/theme9/webresources/choice.shtml
Contents of the Dead Man's Pocket	Jack Finney	Course 5 Pages 199–211	http://www.glencoe.com/sec/literature/course/course5/unit1/theme2/webresources/contents.shtml
The Gift in Wartime	Tran Mong Tu	American Literature Page 389	http://www.glencoe.com/sec/literature/course/amlit/unit3/theme4/webresources/wartime.shtml
I've Seen the Promised Land	Martin Luther King, Jr.	Course 5 Pages 517–525	http://www.glencoe.com/sec/literature/course/course5/unit2/theme6/webresources/promised.shtml
Lullaby	Leslie Marmon Silko	Course 5 Pages 330–338	http://www.glencoe.com/sec/literature/course/course5/unit1/theme4/webresources/lullaby.shtml
Prime Time	Henry Louis Gates, Jr.	American Literature Pages 1087–1094	http://www.glencoe.com/sec/literature/course/amlit/unit7/theme11/webresources/primetime.shtml
Rain Music	Longhang Nguyen	American Literature Pages 1067–1069	http://www.glencoe.com/sec/literature/course/amlit/unit7/theme11/webresources/music.shtml
from Stay Alive, My Son	Pin Yathay	American Literature Pages 93–96	http://www.glencoe.com/sec/literature/course/amlit/unit1/theme1/webresources/stayalive.shtml
from Stride Toward Freedom	Martin Luther King, Jr.	American Literature Pages 892–894	http://www.glencoe.com/sec/literature/course/amlit/unit6/theme9/webresources/freedom.shtml
A Swimming Lesson	Jewelle L. Gomez	Course 5 Pages 495–497	http://www.glencoe.com/sec/literature/course/course5/unit2/theme5/webresources/swimming.shtml
That Place Where Ghosts of Salmon Jump	Sherman Alexie	World Literature Pages 1052–1053	http://www.glencoe.com/sec/literature/course/wrldlit/unit6/part1/webresources/salmon.shtml
Thoughts of Hanoi	Nguyen Thi Vinh	World Literature Pages 741–742	http://www.glencoe.com/sec/literature/course/wrldlit/unit4/part2/webresources/hanoi.shtml
Visit to a Small Planet	Gore Vidal	Course 4 Pages 922–946	http://www.glencoe.com/sec/literature/course/course4/unit6/theme12/webresources/smallplanet.shtml
When Heaven and Earth Changed Places	Le Ly Hayslip	World Literature Pages 747–752	http://www.glencoe.com/sec/literature/course/wrldlit/unit4/part2/webresources/earth.shtml
With All Flags Flying	Anne Tyler	Course 5 Pages 115–123	http://www.glencoe.com/sec/literature/course/course5/unit1/theme1/webresources/flags.shtml
from The Woman Warrior	Maxine Hong Kingston	American Literature Pages 1036–1041	http://www.glencoe.com/sec/literature/course/amlit/unit7/theme11/webresources/warrior.shtml
The World is Not a Pleasant Place to Be	Nikki Giovanni	Course 4 Page 477	http://www.glencoe.com/sec/literature/course/course4/unit3/theme6/webresources/theworld.shtml

Unit 10: A Changing Society, 1968–Present

Selection Title	Author	The Reader's Choice Text & Location	Web Link
Appetizer	Robert H. Abel	Course 5 Pages 1016–1025	http://www.glencoe.com/sec/literature/course/course5/unit6/theme12/webresources/appetizer.shtml
As It Is with Strangers	Susan Beth Pfeffer	Course 5 Pages 279–284	http://www.glencoe.com/sec/literature/course/course5/unit1/theme3/webresources/strangers.shtml
Catch the Moon	Judith Ortiz Cofer	Course 5 Pages 63–69	http://www.glencoe.com/sec/literature/course/course5/unit1/theme1/webresources/catch.shtml
Fishing	Joy Harjo	World Literature Pages 1189–1190	http://www.glencoe.com/sec/literature/course/wrldlit/unit6/part2/webresources/fishing.shtml
The Flat of the Land	Diana García	Course 4 Pages 959–966	http://www.glencoe.com/sec/literature/course/course4/unit6/theme12/webresources/flatland.shtml
The House / La Casa	María Herrera-Sobek	American Literature Page 1168	http://www.glencoe.com/sec/literature/course/amlit/unit7/theme12/webresources/casa.shtml
I Was a Skinny Tomboy Kid	Alma Luz Villanueva	Course 4 Pages 456–457	http://www.glencoe.com/sec/literature/course/course4/unit3/theme6/webresources/skinny.shtml
from A Match to the Heart	Gretel Ehrlich	Course 5 Pages 544–550	http://www.glencoe.com/sec/literature/course/course5/unit2/theme6/webresources/match.shtml
Naming Myself	Barbara Kingsolver	American Literature Page 1190	http://www.glencoe.com/sec/literature/course/amlit/unit7/theme12/webresources/myself.shtml
Prologue	Edward Field	Course 4 Page 985	http://www.glencoe.com/sec/literature/course/course4/unit6/theme12/webresources/prologue.shtml
Rain Music	Longhang Nguyen	American Literature Pages 1067–1069	http://www.glencoe.com/sec/literature/course/amlit/unit7/theme11/webresources/music.shtml
Scanning the Heavens for Signs of Life	William J. Broad	Course 4 Pages 951–954	http://www.glencoe.com/sec/literature/course/course4/unit6/theme12/webresources/heavens.shtml
The Sentinel	Arthur C. Clarke	Course 4 Pages 907–915	http://www.glencoe.com/sec/literature/course/course4/unit6/theme12/webresources/sentinel.shtml
A Sound of Thunder	Ray Bradbury	Course 5 Pages 316–325	http://www.glencoe.com/sec/literature/course/course5/unit1/theme4/webresources/soundofthunder.shtml
Traveling Through the Dark	William Stafford	American Literature Page 1143	http://www.glencoe.com/sec/literature/course/amlit/unit7/theme12/webresources/traveling.shtml
The Tuscan Zoo	Lewis Thomas	Course 5 Pages 563–565	http://www.glencoe.com/sec/literature/course/course5/unit2/theme6/webresources/tucson.shtml
The Universe	May Swenson	Course 4 Page 986	http://www.glencoe.com/sec/literature/course/course4/unit6/theme12/webresources/prologue.shtml
from The Way to Rainy Mountain	N. Scott Momaday	American Literature Pages 1054–1059	http://www.glencoe.com/sec/literature/course/amlit/unit7/theme11/webresources/mountain.shtml

Native American People of the Eastern Woodlands

★ BACKGROUND

Native American peoples lived throughout the regions of the North American continent: the North, Pacific Coast, Southwest, Great Plains, and Eastern Woodlands. Stretching west from the Hudson River across what is today New York and southern Ontario and north to Georgian Bay lived one of the powerful Northeastern peoples—those who spoke Iroquoian. Consisting of many nations, all of the Iroquoian people had similar cultures. They lived in longhouses in large towns protected by stockades. The people lived in large kinship groups, or extended families headed by the elder women of each clan. Up to ten related families lived together in each longhouse.

Despite their similar cultures, war often erupted among the Iroquoian groups. In the late 1500s, five of the nations in western New York—the Seneca, Cayuga, Onondaga, Oneida, and Mohawk—formed an alliance to maintain peace. This alliance was later called the Iroquois League or Iroquois Confederacy. Europeans called these five nations the Iroquois, even though other nations spoke Iroquoian as well.

According to Iroquois tradition, Dekanawidah, a shaman or tribal elder, and Hiawatha, a chief of the Mohawk, founded the League. They were worried that war was tearing the five nations apart at a time when the more powerful Huron people threatened them all. The five nations agreed to the Great Binding Law, a constitution that defined how the confederacy worked.

★ STRATEGIES

Have students read *The Iroquois Constitution* on page 55 in Glencoe Literature's *The Reader's Choice: American Literature.* Written by Dekanawidah, *The Iroquois Constitution* presents his ideas about the unity necessary to strengthen the nations of the Iroquois. Presented to the Native American nations by his lifelong friend and more eloquent speaker, Hiawatha, the constitution outlines the land divisions among the groups, calls the leaders of the groups to act as mentors, and defines the symbolism of the five nations:

Five arrows shall be bound together very strong, and each arrow shall represent one nation. As the five arrows are strongly bound, this shall symbolize the complete union of the nations. Thus are the Five Nations united completely and enfolded together, united into one head, one body, and one mind.

After the Iroquois Confederacy was established and his task completed, Dekanawidah mysteriously disappeared.

★ ACTIVITIES

Ask students the following questions, and then have them complete the activity below.

1. Explain the purpose of *The Iroquois Constitution.* *(The constitution was written to outline the beliefs and guidelines that would govern the Iroquois Confederacy.)*

2. How does the quote represent the fears that drove leaders like Dekanawidah and Hiawatha to attempt to unite the Iroquois people? *(They feared that strong groups, like the Huron, would take their land, deplete their natural resources, and overpower their own people. They viewed unity as necessary to achieve strength and survival.)*

3. **Writing Prompt:** Research a political or social group that has broken into factions, thereby weakening the group overall. Assume that you have been assigned to mediate the factions and write a constitution that would protect the interests of all parties involved, yet unite the divisions. Use Dekanawidah's *The Iroquois Constitution* as a model.

The Pilgrims Land at Plymouth

✪ BACKGROUND

On September 16, 1620, 101 Puritans set sail from England on the journey across the Atlantic on the *Mayflower*. The trip took 65 days. Most of the food ran out, many passengers became ill, and one died. Making matters worse, a severe storm blew the small ship off course. Finally, on November 11, the Pilgrims sighted Cape Cod and, facing rough and stormy seas, landed. Although they were not where they expected, the Pilgrims were not completely lost. In 1614, the Virginia Company had hired Captain John Smith to explore the region. The Pilgrims had a copy of John Smith's "Map of New England," and they decided to move across Massachusetts Bay to the area Smith had labeled "Plymouth" on his map.

✪ STRATEGIES

Have students read *Of Plymouth Plantation* on page 69 of Glencoe Literature's *The Reader's Choice: American Literature*. Point out that William Bradford was one of the Separatists who voyaged to Plymouth Rock in 1620. During the long and life-threatening voyage, Bradford helped write the Mayflower Compact to establish the colony's rules of government. Another of his historical documents, *Of Plymouth Plantation,* gives a detailed account of the Pilgrims' experiences aboard the *Mayflower* and in the Plymouth colony. Chapter 9 describes scenes from the harrowing voyage:

> **[T]he winds were so fierce and the seas so high, as they could not bear a knot of sail, but were forced to hull for [several] days together. And in one of them, as they thus lay at hull in a mighty storm, a lusty young man called John Howland . . . was, with a seele of the ship, thrown into sea; but it pleased God that he caught hold of the topsail halyards which hung overboard and ran out at length.**

In Chapter 11, Bradford writes:

> **But that which was most sad and lamentable was, that in two or three months' time half of their company died, especially in January and February, being the depth of winter, and wanting houses and other comforts; being infected with the scurvy and other diseases which this long voyage and their inaccommodate condition had brought upon them.**

Further writings continue to describe the conditions surrounding the colonization of America, with Bradford writing specifically of Squanto's instruction to the Pilgrims in basic survival techniques in the new land.

> **[B]ut Squanto continued with them and was their interpreter and was a special instrument sent of God for their good. . . . He directed them how to set their corn, where to take fish, and to procure other commodities, and was also their pilot to bring them to unknown places for their profit. . . .**

✪ ACTIVITIES

Ask students the following questions, and then have them complete the activity below.

1. Describe the conditions the Pilgrims faced on board the *Mayflower* and discuss their level of preparedness for such conditions. (*Life on the* Mayflower *was perilous. Besides surviving stormy and rough seas, the Pilgrims also faced malnutrition and even starvation. Additionally, the Pilgrims had to endure extreme shifts in temperature and confusion of location and direction while at sea. The Pilgrims were ill-prepared for such a voyage and for life in America because both situations were different from the lives they had led in Europe.*)

2. Predict the impact on the Pilgrims if Squanto had not befriended them. (*Most likely, they would have perished. His instruction equipped the Pilgrims to survive the harsh conditions of New England.*)

3. **Writing Prompt:** Have students assume the point of view of William Bradford as they write advertisements for an English newspaper in the early 1600s. The ads should seek settlers to join the Pilgrims in the colonies and should focus on the type of colonists that William Bradford would have wanted to settle in his colony. Include in your ad the characteristics necessary for survival in the harsh land.

Enslaved Africans in Early America

★ BACKGROUND

From the earliest days of settlement, tobacco was the cash crop of Virginia and Maryland. There was plenty of land for tobacco farmers, but not enough labor to work it. Bacon's Rebellion of 1676 accelerated the already existing trend of using enslaved Africans instead of indentured servants to work the Virginian plantations. Enslaved peoples were cheaper and never had to be freed—thus, the use of enslaved Africans to help run plantations became widespread throughout the South during the late 1700s.

For enslaved Africans, the voyage to America usually began with a march to a European fort on the West African coast. Tied together with ropes around their necks and hands, they were traded to Europeans, branded, and forced aboard a ship. Historians estimate that between 10 and 12 million Africans were enslaved and forcibly transported to the Americas between 1520 and 1870. Roughly 2 million died at sea before reaching the Americas.

★ STRATEGIES

Have students read *The Life of Olaudah Equiano* on page 189 in Glencoe Literature's *The Reader's Choice: American Literature.* West Africans captured Olaudah Equiano from the village of Essaka in West Africa when he was eleven years old. Sold to European traders, Olaudah made the two-month voyage across the Atlantic, known as the Middle Passage, and arrived in Barbados. Purchased by an officer of the British Royal Navy, Olaudah was renamed Gustavus Vassa. He learned to read and write, and purchased his freedom at age 21. Settling in England, he devoted his life to the antislavery movement and recorded his experiences in a powerful autobiography published in 1789, *The Interesting Life of Olaudah Equiano,* or *Gustavus Vassa, the African.*

> The first object which saluted my eyes when I arrived on the coast, was the sea, and a slave ship, which was then riding at anchor, and waiting for its cargo. These filled me with astonishment, which was soon converted into terror, when I was carried on board. . . . I was now persuaded that I had gotten into a world of bad spirits, and that they were going to kill me.

Despite such terror, Equiano was indeed curious and observant of this new world:

> During our passage, I first saw flying fishes, which surprised me very much; they used frequently to fly across the ship, and many of them fell on the deck. I also now first saw the use of the quadrant . . . and one of them . . . willing to gratify my curiosity, made me one day look through it. . . . This heightened my wonder; and I was now more persuaded than ever, that I was in another world, and that everything about me was magic.

Faced with the new horrors of the merchant yard, Equiano writes:

> O, ye nominal Christians! might not an African ask you—Learned you this from your God, who says unto you, Do unto all men as you would men should do unto you? Is it not enough that we are torn from our country and friends, to toil for your luxury and lust of gain? . . . Why are parents to lose their children, brothers their sisters, or husbands their wives? Surely, this is a new refinement in cruelty. . . .

★ ACTIVITIES

Ask students the following questions, and then have them complete the activity below.

1. Equiano survived the Middle Passage while close to 2 million Africans did not. Consider personal characteristics evident in Equiano's writing that demonstrate his instinct for survival. *(Answers may vary but could include that he observed his surroundings and contemplated the interactions among others; he maintained an inquisitive nature; he found beauty in all the horror surrounding him; he drew on his beliefs for strength.)*

2. Describe Equiano's attitude toward the selling of slaves. *(He felt it went against the teachings of the Europeans' God, that it was "a new refinement in cruelty," and that it could not be defended.)*

3. **Writing Prompt:** Write an essay in defense of freedom, explaining at least three reasons that no person should ever own another.

The Townshend Acts

★ BACKGROUND

The Townshend Acts of 1767 were imposed on colonists as the British attempted to raise funds to pay war costs. One of the Townshend Acts was the Revenue Act of 1767, which put new customs duties on goods imported into the colonies. Violators of the Revenue Act had to face trial in pro-British vice-admiralty courts. To assist customs officers in arresting smugglers, the Revenue Act legalized the use of "writs of assistance," or general search warrants. They enabled customs officers to enter any location during the day to look for evidence of smuggling.

Not surprisingly, the Townshend Acts infuriated many colonists. In May 1769, Virginia's House of Burgesses passed the Virginia Resolves, stating that only the House had the right to tax Virginians. Under orders from Britain, Virginia's governor dissolved the House of Burgesses. In response, the leaders of the House of Burgesses—including George Washington, Patrick Henry, and Thomas Jefferson—immediately called the members to a "convention." This convention then passed a nonimportation law, blocking the sale of British goods in Virginia.

★ STRATEGIES

Have students read "Speech to the Second Virginia Convention" on page 147 of Glencoe Literature's *The Reader's Choice: American Literature*. Lead students to understand why oration ingrained itself as a powerful tool during the years preceding the American Revolution. A famous orator was Patrick Henry. He is perhaps most widely known for the phrase, "Give me liberty or give me death," which closed his famous and stirring "Speech to the Second Virginia Convention." Powerfully structured to ask and answer a series of forthright questions concerning British treatment of the colonists, Henry admits the magnitude of the actions of the House leaders:

The question before the house is one of awful moment to this country. For my own part, I consider it as nothing less than a question of freedom or slavery.

Numerous exclamations mark the final paragraphs of the speech as Henry calls the Virginia Convention to join with the colonists in Massachusetts who were already engaged in open opposition to the British:

Gentlemen may cry peace, peace—but there is no peace. The war is actually begun! The next gale that sweeps from the North will bring to our ears the clash of resounding arms! Our brethren are already in the field! Why stand we here idle? . . . Is life so dear, or peace so sweet, as to be purchased at the price of chains and slavery? Forbid

it, Almighty God! I know not what course others may take; but as for me, give me liberty, or give me death!

Soon the battles of the American Revolution would rage around the people of Virginia. Henry was elected in 1776 to be the first governor of the commonwealth under its new constitution, and his ability to stir up and unite people served Virginians well during this most turbulent and necessary period.

★ ACTIVITIES

Ask students the following questions, and then have them complete the activity below.

1. In the closing line, Henry states two choices he sees for himself. What are they? *(freedom from British rule or death)*

2. Do you agree or disagree with Henry's statement that revolution was "nothing less than a question of freedom or slavery"? Explain your answer. *(Answers may vary, but most students will agree. Reasons may include that the British had sent soldiers to monitor daily actions of the colonists; through the writs of assistance, the colonists could be searched and sent to England for trial; and the colonists were not permitted to govern themselves.)*

3. **Writing Prompt:** Write an expanded definition of "liberty." Include in your definition what liberty meant to the colonists as well as what it means to you.

George Washington—Leader of the Continental Army

★ BACKGROUND

In 1783 General George Washington arrived in Newburgh, New York to meet with and convince officers of the Continental Army not to rebel against the government. Deeply in debt and angry with Congress, the officers had petitioned Congress for back pay and pensions. Congress could not pay the interest on its loans, meet the army payroll, or raise the money it needed because the states refused to grant Congress the power to tax. The members of Congress then drew the officers into a scheme to threaten the states with a military takeover unless they agreed to give Congress the power to tax. Several top officers became involved and sent an angry letter to other officers arguing that the time had come to take action.

When Washington read a copy of the letter, he called a meeting of all high-ranking officers at Newburgh. When he arrived at the meeting, he was met with hostility. In his speech, he criticized the "insidious purposes" of the letter, which threatened the separation between "military and civil" affairs. Congress, he said, might move slowly, but it would address their concerns. Reminded through the words and actions of Washington of the battles they had fought together and the ideals they shared, the officers quickly pledged their loyalty to Congress. Washington's integrity had preserved a basic principle—that the army should not interfere in politics.

—Quotes from *The Forging of the Union*

★ STRATEGIES

Have students read "To His Excellency, General Washington" on page 178 of Glencoe Literature's *The Reader's Choice: American Literature.* Explain that when General George Washington took command of the Continental Army in 1775, Phyllis Wheatley, an enslaved woman, wrote and forwarded to him this poem of tribute. Rich with allusions to Greek mythology, Wheatley personifies America as "Columbia," a goddess of liberty:

Columbia's scenes of glorious toils I write.
While freedom's cause her anxious breast alarms,
She flashes dreadful in refulgent arms.

Building a picture of America's ensuing fight with Britain, Wheatley's hope for the outcome is clear:

Fix'd are the eyes of nations on the scales,
For in their hopes Columbia's arm prevails.

Wheatley not only supports the colonies, but also extols the virtues and leadership of George Washington:

Fam'd for thy valour, for thy virtues more,
Hear every tongue thy guardian aid implore!

Wheatley uses a series of heroic couplets to pay homage to Washington and America, underscoring her admiration for the colonies and one of its great leaders. Commonly used in epic poems to describe heroes and their great deeds, the heroic couplet consists of two rhyming lines built with iambic pentameter (10 syllables; unstressed followed by stressed) to create rhythm.

★ ACTIVITIES

Ask students the following questions, and then have them complete the activity below.

1. Consider your readings about George Washington. List his personality traits that stirred great respect among early Americans for this army general. *(integrity, persistence, honesty, patriotism, bravery, cunning)*

2. Wheatley's poem gives the reader insight to her feelings about America and General Washington. Summarize the major opinions expressed in her poem. *(She reveres Washington's bravery and ability to lead, she believes the quest for freedom is heroic and worthy, and she believes America is capable of success.)*

3. **Writing Prompt:** Use Wheatley's poem as a model to create a tribute to a personal hero. Attempt to effectively use one of the literary techniques employed by Wheatley.

War of 1812

★BACKGROUND

James Madison assumed the office of president from Thomas Jefferson in the midst of an international crisis. Tensions that had been created as Britain forced impressments on American ships were rising. Madison asked Congress to pass the Non-Intercourse Act. This act reopened trade with all nations except France and Britain, but authorized the president to reopen trade with either France or Britain, whichever one removed its restrictions on trade first. The idea was to play France and Britain against each other and avoid war; however, the plan failed. In May 1810, Congress tried again to open trade with both Britain and France with Macon's Bill Number Two. It stated that if either nation agreed to drop its restrictions on trade, the United States would stop importing goods from the other nation. America struck an agreement with France, and Madison's strategy eventually worked. By early 1812, the refusal of the United States to buy British goods had begun to hurt the British economy. British merchants and manufacturers began to pressure their government to repeal its restrictions on trade. Finally, in June 1812, Britain ended all restrictions on American trade. The British decision, however, came too late. Two days later, the British learned that the United States Congress had declared war on Great Britain.

★STRATEGIES

Lead students in a discussion of means one could employ to preserve important artifacts of American culture slated for destruction. Discuss peaceful protests, petitions, speeches, mass mailings, television commercials, and letters to the editor as possible means to publicize and gain support for a cause. Explain that in 1830, Oliver Wendell Holmes wrote a persuasive poem, published it in the *Boston Daily Advertiser,* and, through the interest and support he gained, saved an important American artifact, the USS *Constitution,* from destruction. Nicknamed *Old Ironsides* by sailors who had witnessed the frigate's weathering of British battering during the War of 1812, the USS *Constitution* held importance as one of the earliest American symbols of patriotism and power. Have students read the selection "Old Ironsides" by Oliver Wendell Holmes on page 225 of Glencoe Literature's *The Reader's Choice: American Literature,* and consider Holmes's imagery:

Ay, tear her tattered ensign down!
Long has it waved on high,
And many an eye has danced to see
That banner in the sky. . . .

In the second stanza, the imagery becomes nationally symbolic and personal as it reminds Americans of the contributions of sailors and their ship to American causes:

Her deck, once red with heroes' blood,
Where knelt the vanquished foe. . . .

Holmes's poem effectively advertised the ship's impending destruction and triggered an outpouring of support that preserved the ship, which is currently docked at the Charleston Navy Yard in Massachusetts.

★ACTIVITIES

Ask students the following questions, and then have them complete the activity below.

1. Explain Holmes's purpose in writing and publishing "Old Ironsides." *(Holmes wanted to publicize the ship's impending destruction and stimulate the support of others to preserve an artifact of American history.)*

2. State and explain at least two reasons that Holmes's cause was realized. *(Students' answers may vary. Holmes appealed to the emotions of Americans, reminding them of the protection the ship offered during past wars. He appealed to the American conscience by referring to those who wanted to destroy the ship as "harpies" who were plucking something beautiful and important from the ocean.)*

3. **Writing prompt:** Choose a symbol or aspect of American culture that is being threatened. Write persuasively about the subject, appealing to the emotions and consciences of Americans to support your cause.

Growth in the North

✱BACKGROUND

Francis C. Lowell, a leader in the expansion of industry in the North, opened a series of mills in northeastern Massachusetts beginning in 1814 and introduced mass production of cotton cloth to the United States. His Boston Manufacturing Company built residences for workers in the Massachusetts town named after Lowell and employed thousands of workers. By 1840 scores of textile factories sprang up throughout the Northeast. Industrialists soon applied factory techniques to the production of lumber, shoes, leather, wagons and carts, and other products. A wave of inventions and technological innovations continued to spur the nation's industrial growth. Industrial expansion churned in the Northeast with such innovations as the machination of interchangeable parts, the sewing machine, tin can preservation of food, and the telegraph. Thousands of people from farms and villages were drawn to towns in search of factory jobs with higher wages, and many city populations doubled or tripled. In 1820 only two American cities boasted more than 100,000 residents. By 1860 eight cities had reached that size.

✱STRATEGIES

Explain to the students that the people of New England contributed not only to the industrialization of our country, but also to the development of a body of American literature. Washington Irving, a New Englander, was one of the first American writers to gain international fame when he published *A History of New York* (1809) under the pseudonym Diedrich Knickerbocker. Most students will be more familiar with Irving's "The Legend of Sleepy Hollow" and "Rip Van Winkle." Have students read "The Devil and Tom Walker" on page 203 of Glencoe Literature's *The Reader's Choice: American Literature*. Prepare them for reading by establishing the historical background of the story, which is set in New England in the early 1700s. As the decline of Puritanism became more widespread, increasing numbers of people became concerned with the acquisition of wealth. Instruct students that allusions are references in literature to people, places, and events from history, religion, or other pieces of literature. This selection alludes to treasure supposedly buried by Captain William Kidd (1645–1701) and the Faustian legend, which deals with selling one's soul to the Devil. This selection presents a fictional husband and wife, both miserly and greedy:

Whatever the woman could lay hands on she hid away. . . . Her husband was continually prying about to detect her secret hoards.

When Tom, the husband, unsuspectingly converses with the Devil, he returns to tell his wife of the terms of the agreement the "wild huntsman" offered: his soul and service in return for the treasure of Captain Kidd. When Tom refuses to strike the deal with the Devil, the wife carries the family treasures into the woods in search of the "black miner," never to be seen again. Eventually, Tom strikes a deal with the Devil. After he accumulates wealth and grows old, he regrets his decision. He turns to religion for protection; however, during a moment of weakness, his promise is kept and Tom is taken by the Devil.

✱ACTIVITIES

Ask students the following questions, and then have them complete the activity below.

1. Discuss the Faustian theme and the possible reasons it appears in many literary selections. *(The Faustian legend stems from German literature and is credited to Johann Wolfgang von Goethe. Stated simply, the Faustian legend means one sacrifices spiritual goals for material gain. It is a popular legend because it exemplifies the weakness of human character—one of the universal literary themes.)*

2. Define the term *allusion* and explain its contribution to this literary selection. *(Allusion is an implied or stated reference to a person, place, or event from history, literature, or religion. The allusions to Captain Kidd and Faust deepen the story and provide motive for the actions of the characters.)*

3. **Writing Prompt:** Determine the message, or theme, Irving creates in this selection and write a literary analysis, stating the theme in the first paragraph and tracing its development in subsequent paragraphs. Incorporate quotes from the story to support your statements.

American Writers Emerge

✪BACKGROUND

In the mid to late 1800s, the nation's artists and writers set out to create uniquely American works that celebrated the people, history, and natural beauty of the United States. Some of the most notable include James Fenimore Cooper, who wrote *The Last of the Mohicans* (1826). Nathaniel Hawthorne, a New England customs official, wrote over 100 tales and novels, with *The Scarlet Letter* (1850) being one of his most famous. Herman Melville, another New Englander, wrote the great *Moby Dick* (1851). Edgar Allen Poe, a poet and short story writer, achieved fame as a Gothic writer of terror and mystery.

✪STRATEGIES

Build on the information above by pointing out to students that as industrialization and its by-product, population growth, were sweeping New England, this part of the country was also home to an emerging literary and religious movement known as Transcendentalism. Ralph Waldo Emerson and Henry David Thoreau— philosophers, writers, lecturers, and political activists— are both recognized as the first agents of a genuine "literary movement" in America. Have students read pages 238–261 in Glencoe Literature's *The Reader's Choice: American Literature.* Help students define Transcendentalism as a literary movement that recognized the unity of God, man, and nature. Emerson outlines the basic tenets of Transcendentalism in his long essay entitled "Nature":

> **In the woods, we return to reason and faith. There I feel that nothing can befall me in life,—no disgrace, no calamity (leaving me my eyes), which nature cannot repair. Standing on the bare ground . . . all mean egotism vanishes. I become a transparent eyeball; I am nothing; I see all; the currents of the Universal Being circulate through me; I am part or parcel of God.**

Of course, such free thinkers as the transcendentalists held political beliefs, many that were quite unpopular among mainstream America. Explain to students that transcendentalists believed strongly in nonconformity. Emerson writes in "Self-Reliance":

> **Society everywhere is in conspiracy against the manhood of every one of its members. Society is a joint-stock company in which the members agree for the better securing of his bread to each shareholder, to surrender the liberty and culture of the eater. . . . Whoso would be a man must be a nonconformist.**

Henry David Thoreau embraced and furthered the transcendentalist notions instigated by Emerson. A committed abolitionist and philosopher, Thoreau wrote about his observations of nature in "Walden." This long essay shares the name of Emerson's Massachusetts pond, which is where Thoreau lived for more than two years to distance himself from civilization. Thoreau writes about his purpose at Walden:

> **I went to the woods because I wished to live deliberately, to front only the essential facts of life, and see if I could not learn what it had to teach, and not, when I came to die, discover that I had not lived.**

Encourage your students to examine both the merits and pitfalls of the transcendentalist movement.

✪ACTIVITIES

Ask students the following questions, and then have them complete the activity below.

1. Define Transcendentalism. *(Transcendentalism was a literary movement stating that God, man, and nature were one, each one reflected and unified by the other.)*

2. Why were transcendentalists operating outside of mainstream America? *(At this point in history, most Americans were busy industrializing the nation and supporting America's young government. The transcendentalists were focused instead on self-reliance, nature, and civil disobedience.)*

3. **Writing Prompt:** Read an excerpt from Thoreau's "Civil Disobedience." Write an opinion essay stating your perspective of historic or modern civil disobedience. Quote Thoreau to prove or disprove your points.

Populating California

✪BACKGROUND

In the 1840s, Americans headed west to the frontier states of the Midwest and the rich lands of California and Oregon. Hoping to attract more settlers, Juan Bautista Alvarado, governor of California, granted 50,000 acres in the Sacramento Valley to John Sutter, a German immigrant. There Sutter built a trading post and cattle ranch. Sutter's Fort—as it was called—was often the first stopping point for Americans reaching California. After James Marshall discovered gold in California in 1848, the transformation in the West was immediate and spectacular. Mining towns sprang up overnight and small towns rapidly grew into cities. By the end of 1849, nearly 80,000 people had entered California to seek their fortunes.

✪STRATEGIES

Point out to students that American literature was constantly expanding to mirror the changes occurring in the American landscape. *Regionalism* is writing that attempts to capture the local color of a group of people. Bret Harte was one of the first American writers to capture the local color of the "wild, wild West" by incorporating vernacular, or dialect, into his writing. Have students read the selection "The Outcasts of Poker Flat" on page 476 of Glencoe Literature's *The Reader's Choice: American Literature.* This selection will allow them to recognize local color and to better understand the mercurial atmosphere that often permeated mining towns, where people of all walks of life mixed in rough, lawless, and often violent circumstances:

In point of fact, Poker Flat was "after somebody." It had lately suffered the loss of several thousand dollars, two valuable horses, and a prominent citizen. It was experiencing a spasm of virtuous reaction, quite as lawless and ungovernable as any of the acts that had provoked it. A secret committee had determined to rid the town of all improper persons.

Thus, Poker Flat banishes four of its most notorious characters, one of whom is the gambler John Oakhurst. Instead of striking out on his own, he chooses to become the leader of this motley crew as they head through the Sierras to a neighboring camp called Sandy Bar. After meeting up with a pair of runaway lovers, Tom Simson (a gambling foe of Oakhurst's) and

Piney, the entire group becomes imprisoned in a hut by a relentless snowstorm. When one member of the party dies and provisions dwindle, Oakhurst and Simson forge into the storm to bring help from Poker Flat. Only one character returns to the hut, however, and it is not Oakhurst:

And pulseless and cold, with a derringer by his side and a bullet in his heart, though still calm as in life, beneath the snow lay he who was at once the strongest and yet the weakest of the outcasts of Poker Flat.

✪ACTIVITIES

Ask students the following questions, and then have them complete the activity below.

1. Who often governed the mining towns? Discuss the risk of such self-governing. *(Mining towns were often governed by citizens who "took the law into their own hands." The major risk was that the "bad guys" sometimes undid the "good guys." Additionally, justice fluctuated with the whims of the most powerful people.)*

2. What is the "moral" of this story? *(John Oakhurst acted selflessly by choosing to stay with the people who needed him as opposed to saving himself by striking out on his own. Sometimes, especially when associating with "lawless" people, self-preservation is warranted.)*

3. **Writing Prompt:** Write an alternative ending to this story.

The Underground Railroad

★BACKGROUND

Under the Fugitive Slave Act of 1850, a person claiming that an African American had escaped from slavery had only to point out that person as a runaway to take him or her into custody. Although the Fugitive Slave Act included heavy fines and prison terms for helping a runaway, whites and free African Americans continued their work with the Underground Railroad. This informal but well-organized system, begun in the early 1830s, helped thousands of enslaved persons escape. Members, called "conductors," transported runaways north in secret, gave them shelter and food along the way, and saw them to freedom in the Northern states or Canada with some money for a fresh start.

Dedicated people, many of them African Americans, made dangerous trips into the South to guide enslaved persons along the Underground Railroad to freedom. The most famous of these conductors was Harriet Tubman, herself a runaway. Over and over again, she risked journeys into the slave states to bring out men, women, and children.

★STRATEGIES

Have students read "Swing Low, Sweet Chariot," "Go Down, Moses," and "Follow the Drinking Gourd" on pages 337–339 of Glencoe Literature's *The Reader's Choice: American Literature.* Explain that spirituals served many purposes for the enslaved people of the South. Rooted in oral tradition and passed down from generation to generation, the spirituals first served to preserve their history of ancestry. Later, spirituals were common in worship services as well as in the fields, expressing both religious faith and the desire to live freely. Eventually, prior to the outbreak of the Civil War, spirituals began to be a form of secret code that was sung in the fields to give directions to those wishing to escape. In "Go Down, Moses," building an allusion to the Jews enslaved by the Egyptians in biblical times, "Egypt" refers to the South or slavery:

**Go down, Moses,
'Way down in Egypt's land;
Tell ole Pharaoh
Let my people go.**

In "Swing Low, Sweet Chariot," the words "heavenly bound" refer to the North or freedom:

**But still my soul feels heavenly bound;
Coming for to carry me home.**

"Follow the Drinking Gourd" describes a series of free slaves and white sympathizers ready to offer aid to fugitive slaves along the Underground Railroad:

**The river bank will make a very good road,
The dead trees will show you the way,
Left foot, peg foot traveling on
Follow the drinking gourd.**

Overall, the spirituals proved to be important to the strength, courage, and freedom of the enslaved people.

★ACTIVITIES

Ask students the following questions, and then have them complete the activity below.

1. Identify three purposes of spirituals. *(religious worship, communication, preservation of history)*

2. Describe the mood or emotion often created by spirituals. *(Spirituals were hopeful and deeply expressive. They helped maintain the focus and strength of a deprived group of people. Spirituals also helped create a mood of courage and trust in one another and the Underground Railroad.)*

3. **Writing Prompt:** The spirituals were inspiring to the enslaved persons. Think about a song that inspires and motivates you. Write a paragraph about the song and the impact it has had on you.

The Battle of Shiloh

★ BACKGROUND

Early on April 6, 1862, Confederate forces launched a surprise attack on General Grant's troops camped near Pittsburgh Landing, Tennessee, about 20 miles (32 km) north of Corinth near a small church named Shiloh. Although the Union troops were forced back, Grant managed to assemble a defensive line that held off repeated Southern attacks.

When the battle ended, several of Grant's commanders advised him to retreat. Grant replied: "Retreat? No. I propose to attack at daylight and whip them." Grant went on the offensive the next morning, surprising the Confederates and forcing General Beauregard, their commander, to order a retreat. The Battle of Shiloh stunned people in both the North and the South. Twenty thousand troops had been killed or wounded, more than in any other battle up to that point.

★ STRATEGIES

Read with students "An Occurrence at Owl Creek Bridge" on page 368 of Glencoe Literature's *The Reader's Choice: American Literature*. Explain that the author, Ambrose Bierce, was a soldier who fought in several Civil War battles. He joined the army to escape an unhappy childhood and a less than promising future. After the war, Bierce became a journalist and author, often drawing on his experiences as a soldier to provide the ideas for his stories. "An Occurrence at Owl Creek Bridge," the fictionalized account of a Southern gentleman's death, is befittingly set at Shiloh, the battle site that saw the wounding or death of more than 20,000 soldiers. Bierce fought at Shiloh and uses third-person narration to create a 35-year-old man who is facing death by hanging. His crime was in aiding the Southern cause by sabotaging a bridge to delay the advancement of Northern troops:

> **He was a civilian, if one might judge from his habit, which was that of a planter. His features were good . . . and had a kindly expression which one would hardly have expected in one whose neck was in the hemp.**

Acutely aware of all that is happening around him, the noosed man, Peyton Farquhar, fantasizes of saving himself and returning home to his wife and children:

> **"If I could free my hands," he thought, "I might throw off the noose and spring into the stream. By diving, I could evade the bullets and, swimming vigorously, reach the bank, take to the woods and get away home."**

Farquhar then lives out his dream. Struggling to escape both the strangling noose and the soldiers' bullets, he imagines himself walking 30 miles to his farm and, finally, being taken into the arms of his wife. Suddenly, however, just as the fictional Farquhar is jolted from his revelry by his fall into the air, so, too, the reader is jolted from revelry with the announcement in the last paragraph:

> **Peyton Farquhar was dead; his body, with a broken neck, swung gently from side to side beneath the timbers of the Owl Creek bridge.**

★ ACTIVITIES

Ask students the following questions, and then have them complete the activity below.

1. Describe Farquhar's fantasy as he waits to die by hanging. *(Farquhar fantasizes about escaping the noose, swimming to shore, walking 30 miles to reach his home, and embracing his wife.)*

2. Explain the events that brought Farquhar to his death. *(A Union scout who was dressed as a Confederate scout tricked Farquhar. The scout revealed information about repairs being made at Owl Creek Bridge to allow for the advancement of Northern troops. Farquhar sabotaged the bridge, was caught, and was sentenced to death.)*

3. **Writing Prompt:** Bierce uses a series of similes—a comparison between two unlike things using *like, as,* or *than*—to describe Farquhar's heightened sense of awareness during the moments before his death. Use similes to describe a common event in slow motion, such as the sloshing of a washing machine.

The Postwar South

★BACKGROUND

The South of 1865 bore little resemblance to the South of 1861. Large areas of the former Confederacy lay in ruins. A traveler on a railroad journey through the South described the region as a "desolated land," adding, "Every village and station we stopped at presented an array of ruined walls and chimneys standing useless and solitary."

Union troops and cannons had left few Southern cities untouched. Describing Columbia, the capital of South Carolina, a Northern reporter noted, "Two-thirds of the buildings in the place were burned, including . . . everything in the business portion. Not a store, office, or shop escaped."

The devastation had left the South's economy in a state of collapse. The value of land had fallen significantly. Confederate money was worthless. Roughly two-thirds of the transportation system lay in ruins, with dozens of bridges destroyed and miles of railroad twisted and rendered useless. Most dramatically of all, the emancipation of African Americans had deprived planters of an estimated four billion dollars they had invested in slaveholding. It had also thrown the agricultural system into chaos. Until the South developed a new system to replace enslaved labor, it could not maintain its agricultural output.

★STRATEGIES

Instruct students to read the selections of poetry by Walt Whitman on pages 403–415 in Glencoe Literature's *The Reader's Choice: American Literature.* Explain that Whitman is often called America's poet. During the Civil War, Whitman's brother suffered wounds, and Whitman traveled to Virginia to care for him. While there, he offered care and sympathy to Confederate and Union soldiers alike. In "A Sight in Camp in the Daybreak Gray and Dim," Whitman captured the "every man" of the war:

Who are you elderly man so gaunt and grim . . . ?
Who are you sweet boy with cheeks yet blooming?
Then to the third . . . I think this is the face of
Christ himself, Dead and divine and brother of
all, and here again he lies.

Later, following the Civil War, the United States experienced economic growth and social change, and Whitman imagined Americans, as opposed to Europeans, breaking free from conventional ways of life and following their own visions. Ask students to pay special attention to "I Hear America Singing" and consider how this poem mirrors the activities of the United States in the aftermath of the Civil War:

I hear America singing, the varied carols I hear,
. . . .

Each singing what belongs to him or her and to
none else,
The day what belongs to the day—at night the
party of young fellows, robust, friendly,
Singing with open mouths their strong melodious
songs.

From the carpenter to the mechanic to the mother, Whitman celebrates the diverse unification of Americans in this poem.

★ACTIVITIES

Ask students the following questions, and then have them complete the activity below.

1. Consider the term "diverse unification" as an oxymoron, or seemingly contradictory term. Explain America's diverse unification. *(Answers will vary. America accepts people of all races, cultures, religions, and professions. Yet when necessary, such as after September 11, 2001, diversity gives way to unification, and Americans stand strongly as one.)*

2. Discuss diverse unification following the Civil War. *(The country had to be rebuilt. Americans contributed as they could to unite the country and rebuild it to be stronger than ever before.)*

3. **Writing Prompt:** Select one of Whitman's poems and use it as a model for creating an original poem celebrating America's diversity.

Relocation

✪BACKGROUND

In 1867 Congress formed an Indian Peace Commission in an attempt to end the growing conflict with Native Americans on the Great Plains. The commission proposed creating two large reservations on the Plains, one for the Sioux and another for southern Plains Indians. The army would deal with any groups that refused to report or remain there. Those who did move to reservations faced much the same conditions that drove the Dakota Sioux to violence—poverty, despair, and the corrupt practices of white traders. Another obstacle to peace on the reservations was the government's failure to fulfill its promises. Treaties signed in this period pledged that the land set aside for Native Americans would remain theirs, but within a few decades, most of the land was in the hands of the white settlers.

In 1877 members of the Nez Perce, led by Chief Joseph, refused to be moved from their ancestral lands to a smaller reservation in Idaho. When the army came to relocate them, they fled their homes and embarked on a flight of more than 1,300 miles that took them eastward through Yellowstone National Park, established in 1872 as the nation's first national park. General William Tecumseh Sherman, who was vacationing there at the time, summoned the U.S. Cavalry to pursue the Nez Perce into Montana. Finally, in October 1877, after losing much of his band in a series of battles, Chief Joseph surrendered and his followers were exiled to Oklahoma.

✪STRATEGIES

Have students read "I Will Fight No More Forever" by Chief Joseph on page 514 in Glencoe Literature's *The Reader's Choice: American Literature*. Explain to students that Chief Joseph's group had maintained peace with Anglo settlers for 70 years—until the U.S. government began reclaiming all of the land it had ceded to the Nez Perce in an 1855 treaty. Chief Joseph attempted to take his people to Canada in 1877 to avoid the forced relocation of his tribe. He did not want his people to be imprisoned on a reservation:

I have asked some of the great white chiefs where they get their authority to say to the Indian that he shall stay in one place, while he sees white men going where they please. They can not tell me.

For more than three months, he led approximately 200 warriors and their families toward Canada. The warriors fought off federal troops repeatedly, but when the group was only 40 miles from Canada, they found themselves surrounded. Chief Joseph chose to surrender:

It is cold and we have no blankets. The little children are freezing to death. My people, some of them, have run away to the hills and have no blankets, no food; no one knows where they are—perhaps freezing to death. I want to have time to look for my children and see how many I can

find. . . . Hear me, my chiefs. I am tired; my heart is sick and sad. From where the sun now stands I will fight no more forever.

As reflected in his words, Chief Joseph's primary concern was for the lives of his people. Eventually, Chief Joseph was taken to a reservation in Washington, where it is said he died of a broken heart.

✪ACTIVITIES

Ask students the following questions, and then have them complete the activity below.

1. Evaluate Chief Joseph's decision to flee and fight. State and support your opinion of his actions. *(Students' answers will vary. Some students will say he made the right decision—his people wanted their freedom and the United States acted against the treaty that offered protection to the Nez Perce. Others will say he made the wrong decision—he should have agreed to the demands of the U.S. government and sought to negotiate a peaceful settlement to the treaty issues.)*

2. Why did Chief Joseph surrender? *(Chief Joseph surrendered because his people were cold, hungry, and dying; members of his group were scattered; and he was tired and deeply disturbed by the condition of his people.)*

3. **Writing Prompt:** Using Chief Joseph's speech as a model, write about a time when you had to defend yourself, either physically or verbally.

Women's Rights

★BACKGROUND

Although the period following the Civil War saw tremendous industrial growth in America, it also was a period of social unrest. Freed African Americans and women both sought a place for themselves in the country. Women were joining the masses working in factories, but most women could not join the AFL because they were classified as unskilled workers. New unions arose to represent these women. Mary Jones, who became the famous labor organizer "Mother Jones," and Polish immigrant Rose Schneiderman both worked to improve conditions for women.

★STRATEGIES

Women's rights became a major social and political concern in the United States following the Civil War, but it had been a concern of some women long before the Civil War. Have students read "And Ain't I a Woman?" by Sojourner Truth on page 345 in Glencoe Literature's *The Reader's Choice: American Literature.* An escaped slave, Sojourner Truth (who eventually took the name Isabella Van Wagener) began her career as a minister. She began to weave the antislavery message into her sermons and eventually adopted the cause of women's rights. She focused heavily on the right of women to vote and delivered perhaps her most famous speech to the Ohio Women's Rights Convention in 1851. Direct and forceful, Truth opens her persuasive speech by stating:

Well, children, where there is so much racket there must be something out of kilter. I think that 'twixt the Negroes of the South and the women at the North, all talking about rights, the white men will be in a fix soon.

Point out to students that Truth effectively asks and answers a repetitive question to emphasize her point:

Nobody ever helps me into carriages, or over mud-puddles, or gives me any best place! And ain't I a woman? Look at me. Look at my arm. I have ploughed and planted, and gathered into barns, and no man could head me! And ain't I a woman?

She closes her short but powerful speech by emphasizing that a woman gave birth to the first man, setting the world in motion, and that the men who dominate the country should allow women to "get it right side up again!" The rights of minorities became a social concern before, and grew even stronger after, the Civil War. Outspoken women and African Americans like Sojourner Truth helped to change the complexion of the country by bringing attention and supporters to the cause of women's rights.

★ACTIVITIES

Ask students the following questions, and then have them complete the activity below.

1. What was the purpose of Sojourner Truth's speech to the Women's Rights Convention in 1851? What methods does she use in her speech to achieve this purpose? *(The purpose of Sojourner Truth's speech was to call attention to the sheer number of enslaved people and women who lived in the country. She used questions to emphasize the contributions women and enslaved African Americans made to the country and drove her point home by alluding to the birth to Christ. She closed her speech with a simple and direct statement—women want to make things right in the world and men better let them.)*

2. Who was Truth trying to persuade in her speech and how does she want them to act? *(She was trying to persuade white men. She wanted them to treat women and African Americans equally.)*

3. **Writing Prompt:** Select the point of view of a woman, enslaved African American, or white man hearing Truth's speech and write a response. Be certain to respond directly to the major points in her speech.

Realism in Literature

✪BACKGROUND

Just as Darwin had looked at the natural world scientifically, a new movement in art and literature known as realism attempted to portray people realistically instead of idealizing them as romantic artists had done. Realism in literature reflected theories emerging in the social sciences, especially history and sociology. Writers as well as artists attempted to capture their world as they saw it. Mark Twain, a Missouri native whose real name was Samuel Clemens, wrote his masterpiece, *The Adventures of Huckleberry Finn,* in 1884. In this novel, the main character, Huck, and his friend Jim, an escaped slave, float down the Mississippi River on a raft. Through their innocent eyes, readers gain a piercing view of American society in the pre-Civil War era. Twain wrote in local dialect and indulged his lively sense of humor.

✪STRATEGIES

Have students read "The Celebrated Jumping Frog of Calaveras County" by Mark Twain on page 462 of Glencoe Literature's *The Reader's Choice: American Literature.* Quoted by Ken Burns of the Public Broadcasting System, Mark Twain said, "I was sorry to have my name mentioned as one of the great authors because they have a habit of dying off. Chaucer is dead, so is Shakespeare, and I'm not feeling very well myself." Despite Twain's humorous perspective on his station in life, both the critics and the American public consider Twain to be the "Lincoln of our literature." During the Civil War, Twain traveled west to seek his fortune. While there, he wrote "The Celebrated Jumping Frog of Calaveras County," which is based on a tale Twain actually heard while visiting Angel's Camp. This tall tale uses a "story frame." An unnamed first-person narrator inquires of garrulous Simon Wheeler information about Leonidas Smiley—the supposed friend of a friend. Simon Wheeler, detecting a captive audience, launches into a tale about the gambling *Jim* Smiley.

Why, it never made no difference to *him*—he would bet on *any* thing—the dangdest feller. Parson Walker's wife laid very sick once, for a good while, and it seemed as if they warn't going to save her. . . . [A]nd Smiley, before he thought, says, "Well, I'll risk two-and-a-half that she don't [live], any way."

Rich with dialect and colloquialisms, the tall tale captures the local color of the mining camps, as in this passage describing a horse race:

They used to give her two or three hundred yards start, and then pass her under way; but always at the fag-end [last part] of the race she'd get excited and desperate-like, and come cavorting [running playfully] and straddling up, and scattering her legs around limber. . . .

Simon Wheeler's yarn ends with Jim Smiley finally being outsmarted when his notorious jumping frog is filled with buckshot (unknown to Jim, of course), which causes him to lose a bet. The story frame ends with the narrator deciding that Jim Smiley is fictitious, and that he had been set up by his friend to become Simon Wheeler's lone audience.

✪ACTIVITIES

Ask students the following questions, and then have them complete the activity below.

1. How does the structure of the story allow Twain to capture the local color while appealing to a variety of audiences? *(The story is written from the perspective of a narrator. The narrator is a refined "easterner" who conveys the stories of semiliterate "westerners," Jim Smiley and Simon Wheeler.)*

2. Describe the impact intended for the audience through the use of dialect, colloquialisms, and exaggeration. *(Twain hoped to make his audience laugh.)*

3. **Writing Prompt:** Write two or more examples of humorous exaggerations that you have heard, and explain why you think each one is funny.

Racial Discrimination

✪BACKGROUND

Beginning around 1890, federal and congressional support for reform in the South had weakened. White Southerners, however, continued to fear that African Americans might join politically with poor whites and weaken the power of the Democratic Party. Southern legislators began to pass discriminatory laws aimed at forcing African Americans into a permanent condition of social, political, and economic inferiority. The new discriminatory measures harmed African Americans in two ways—by depriving them of their right to vote and by enforcing segregation, or separation of the races.

✪STRATEGIES

Have students read "We Wear the Mask" by Paul Laurence Dunbar on page 544 in Glencoe Literature's *The Reader's Choice: American Literature*. Dunbar is credited with saying "I know why the caged bird sings!" which later become the title of a best-selling novel by author Maya Angelou. Dunbar's understanding of his words is certainly reflected in his writing. Dunbar was one of the first African American writers to attain national recognition. As the son of formerly enslaved parents, he grew up in a world that was a mixture of newfound freedom and remembrance of slavery days, both of which were confused by laws that were creating racial discrimination and segregation. The complexities of the lives of African Americans at this time in American history is clearly evident in the words of one of Dunbar's most prolific poems, "We Wear the Mask":

> We wear the mask that grins and lies,
> It hides our cheeks and shades our eyes,—
> This debt we pay to human guile;
> With torn and bleeding hearts we smile,
> And mouth with myriad subtleties.

Oppressed by lawful discriminatory measures, African Americans hid their realities behind masks of obedience and subservience, while their souls were tortured:

> We smile, but, O Great Christ, our cries
> To thee from tortured souls arise.

> We sing, but oh the clay is vile
> Beneath our feet, and long the mile;
> But let the world dream otherwise,
>   We wear the mask!

Dunbar is known for writing pastoral poems describing life before the Civil War, as well as poems expressing pride in African Americans, often lamenting their thwarted efforts to live and create freely.

✪ACTIVITIES

Ask students the following questions, and then have them complete the activity below.

1. Reread "We Wear the Mask." State the reason African Americans felt the need to hide their true feelings and opinions. (*Legislators created many unfair laws that resulted in both legal and illegal punishments that affected the family and friends of the "offender." In order to protect themselves, family members, and friends, African American abided by the unjust laws and hid their true opinions.*)

2. Describe the feelings African Americans had to hide. (*African Americans had to hide their anger over these unjust laws of discrimination and segregation passed by Southern legislators. African Americans felt violated by these laws, which were designed to devalue them.*)

3. **Writing Prompt:** Mimic Dunbar's style as you write a poem expressing your opinion of Jim Crow laws.

The Spanish-American War

☆BACKGROUND

Until Spain abolished slavery in 1886, about one-third of the Cuban population was enslaved and forced to work for wealthy landowners on the plantations. In 1868 Cuban rebels declared independence and launched a guerrilla war against Spanish authorities. Lacking internal support, the rebellion collapsed in 1878. Many Cuban rebels then fled to the United States, where they began planning a new revolution. The exiles raised funds from sympathetic Americans, purchased weapons, and trained their troops in preparation for an invasion of Cuba. The rebels launched a new rebellion in February 1895. The revolutionaries seized control of eastern Cuba, declared independence, and formally established the Republic of Cuba in September 1895. Rebels fought to keep control, and they hoped that news of the destruction of American property in Cuba and Spanish atrocities against Cuban citizens would lead to American intervention between Cuba and Spain.

☆STRATEGIES

Have students read "The Open Boat" by Stephen Crane on page 559 in Glencoe Literature's *The Reader's Choice: American Literature*. Explain that in 1897, Stephen Crane was aboard an American ship, the *Commodore*, which was transporting arms to the Cuban rebels who were fighting for independence from Spain. When the *Commodore* sank, Crane and three others survived aboard a ten-foot dinghy. Crane wrote about this event journalistically for a newspaper and a magazine, and eventually fictionalized the account and entitled it "The Open Boat." Crane's tale is of four crewmen who lose their ship and must spend the night on the open ocean in a dinghy. Crane uses Naturalism, a pessimistic literary movement characterized by a belief that people have little or no control over their lives. The movement focuses on the role of nature in one's life and how the elements of nature—not one's actions—often determine one's fate.

> **"If I am to be drowned—if I am going to be drowned—if I am going to be drowned, why, in the name of the seven mad gods who rule the sea, was I allowed to come thus far and contemplate sand and trees?"**

As the four men waiver between hope and despair, the correspondent contemplates his life experiences and discovers new meaning in past experiences:

> **He had never considered it his affair that a soldier of the Legion lay dying. . . . It was less to him than the breaking of a pencil's point. . . . Now, however, it quaintly came to him as a human,**

> **living thing. . . . He was sorry for the soldier of the Legion who lay dying. . . .**

After a night on the ocean, the men finally determine that they must save themselves. They break through the surf and attempt to swim to shore. The captain, the cook, and the correspondent survive; the oiler perishes, emphasizing the idea that Nature controls man:

> **[T]he wind brought the sound of the great sea's voice to the men on shore, and they felt that they could then be interpreters.**

☆ACTIVITIES

Ask students the following questions, and then have them complete the activity below.

1. Define Naturalism. *(Naturalism is a literary movement that focuses on the role of nature in one's life, often stating that one's fate is determined not by one's actions, but by the elements of nature.)*

2. Identify evidence of Naturalism in "The Open Boat." *(The men were kept from the shore by crashing waves. Without the waves, they would have been ashore shortly after their ship sank and spared a cold and life-threatening night at sea. Also, three of the four men survived their swim to shore while the fourth, who was a strong swimmer, drowned.)*

3. **Writing Prompt:** Write an opinion essay stating and supporting your belief that the outcome of this story is fair or unfair. Compare and contrast your opinion to that held by a Naturalist.

Woman Suffrage

✦BACKGROUND

As the nineteenth century ended, progressives began grassroots movements to change American society. One aspect of social reform was women's rights, with the right to vote being basic to the cause. This movement, known as the suffrage movement, got off to a slow start. Women suffragists were accused of being unfeminine and immoral, which supports the ideas of the time that women belonged in the home. The movement also remained weak because many supporters of woman suffrage were also strong abolitionists. In the years before the Civil War, they preferred to concentrate on abolishing slavery.

After the Civil War, the Republicans in Congress introduced two constitutional amendments to protect the voting rights of African Americans. The Fourteenth Amendment included a section designed to protect the voting rights of all male citizens, while the Fifteenth Amendment protected the right of all male citizens to vote regardless of their race. Several leaders of the woman suffrage movement, including Susan B. Anthony and Elizabeth Cady Stanton, had wanted these amendments worded to give women as well as African Americans the right to vote. They were bitterly disappointed when Republicans and their abolitionist allies refused.

✦STRATEGIES

Have students read "The Story of an Hour" by Kate Chopin on page 525 in Glencoe Literature's *The Reader's Choice: American Literature*. Explain that Kate Chopin lived from 1851 to 1904, thereby witnessing firsthand much of the social unrest of the 1890s. She focused on and wrote about the repression that many women, especially those of the South, experienced. In this selection, Chopin uses dramatic irony to reveal to readers the attitudes held by many women concerning the role that society forced upon them. When Mrs. Mallard, the protagonist of the story, learned of her husband's death, she:

> **. . . did not hear the story as many women have heard the same, with a paralyzed inability to accept its significance. She wept at once, with sudden, wild abandonment. . . . [S]he went to her room alone. She would have no one follow her.**

Following Mrs. Mallard to her room, the reader is privy to her full realization of what her husband's death means to her:

> **There would be no one to live for her during those coming years; she would live for herself. There would be no powerful will bending hers in that blind persistence with which men and women believe they have a right to impose a private will upon a fellow-creature.**

While fully recognizing that she loved her husband, the more overwhelming recognition is that she is "Free! Body and soul free!" As Mrs. Mallory responds to the calls of her sister to leave her room, she "breathed a quick prayer that life might be long." However, as she descends the stairs, the misinformation delivered to her becomes clear when her husband enters the front door. Mrs. Mallard screams and falls to the floor dead, and Chopin closes her masterful tale:

> **When the doctors came they said she had died of heart disease—of joy that kills.**

✦ACTIVITIES

Ask students the following questions, and then have them complete the activity below.

1. Explain the insight the reader gains through Chopin's use of dramatic irony. *(The reader fully understands Mrs. Mallard's feelings of repression. The reader understands that while Mrs. Mallard loved her husband, she felt terribly repressed by his will for her. She was excited that she would no longer have to bend to his will. When this excitement was jerked from her, she died.)*

2. Identify the factions of the population at the turn of the nineteenth century that would have been outraged by Chopin's feminist writings. *(Those who would not have approved of Chopin's writings were white men of power and women who agreed with the male elite.)*

3. **Writing Prompt:** In the story, Mrs. Mallard experiences relief about an unexpected event. Write about a time when you, too, experienced a great sense of relief about an unexpected event.

Advances in Warfare

★BACKGROUND

World War I devastated Europe and claimed millions of lives. Terrible destruction resulted from a combination of old-fashioned strategies, new technologies, and battles fought on two fronts—one in Eastern Europe and one in the west. Along the Western Front, the Allies and Germans engaged in trench warfare, which consisted mainly of quick rushes against enemy positions. Bayonet-wielding soldiers scrambled to hurl hand grenades into the enemy trenches. Defenders employing machine guns could cut down enemy attackers and easily repel assaults. In addition to the machine gun, newer weapons also added to the carnage. In April 1915, the Germans first used poison gas, and the fumes caused vomiting, blindness, and suffocation. In 1916 the British introduced the tank into battle. These first tanks were slow and cumbersome, but they could roll over barbed wire and trenches and helped troops to move more easily through "no man's land." World War I also saw the first use of airplanes in combat, which were eventually used to drop small bombs. As technology advanced, they also attached machine guns to aircraft to engage in deadly air battles known as dogfights.

★STRATEGIES

Have students read Ernest Hemingway's short story "In Another Country" on page 680 in Glencoe Literature's *The Reader's Choice: American Literature.* Point out that Hemingway's style is journalistic in nature, much like Stephen Crane's in "The Open Boat." Explain to students that the literary effect of such a style is an elevated importance in the reader's ability to interpret meaning from the writing. The setting of this selection is Milan, Italy, during World War I. Hemingway uses first-person narration to bring a wounded American soldier in need of rehabilitation into the proximity of wounded Europeans with the same need:

> **We were all at the hospital every afternoon . . . and were all very polite and interested in what was the matter, and sat in the machines that were to make so much difference.**

As is often the case in life, the most unlikely friendships are born from a common ailment, and the group begins comparing war stories and medals. Subsequently, the American detects a change, whether real or perceived, in the attitude of his friends due to the citations around his medal. Thus, the American begins to minimize his wounds and question his ability to effectively soldier:

> **[B]ut we all knew that being wounded, after all, was really an accident. . . . The three with the medals were like hunting-hawks; and I was not a hawk. . . . [T]he three, knew better and so we drifted apart.**

The American's attention then turns to the major whose hand wound is also being rehabilitated through machines at the hospital. Surrounding the machines are pictures of healthy limbs, and the doctor insists that the treatment of the machine guarantees a return to normalcy. The major loses his wife to pneumonia and is devastated. Thus, the end of the story:

> **In front of the machine the major used were three photographs of hands like his that were completely restored. . . . The photographs did not make much difference to the major because he only looked out of the window.**

★ACTIVITIES

Ask students the following questions, and then have them complete the activity below.

1. Explain the symbolism of the resolution of Hemingway's story. *(Students may infer that the photographs were symbolic of hope, and that the major had lost all hope because his wife died.)*

2. Explain the change that occurs in the American's relationship with the three young men. *(The American believes the other soldiers view him as unworthy of the medals, and his relationship with the other soldiers declines.)*

3. **Writing Prompt:** Write an expanded definition of hope. What is it? Where does it come from? How is it lost? Can it be regained?

The Harlem Renaissance

★BACKGROUND

As African Americans from the South built new lives in the North, they gathered together and shared their experiences. In doing so, they created an environment that stimulated artistic development, racial pride, a sense of community, and political organization—an intoxicating atmosphere for artistic expression, which led to a massive creative outpouring. This flowering of African American arts became known as the Harlem Renaissance. Harlem, the largest urban African American community in the country, became a beacon for talented African American writers, musicians, and entertainers. The poet Langston Hughes, one of the most important writers of the Harlem Renaissance, described Harlem's vitality and spirit: "Art took heart from Harlem creativity. Jazz filled the night air . . . and people came from all around after dark to look upon our city within a city, Black Harlem."

★STRATEGIES

Have students turn to page 740 in Glencoe Literature's *The Reader's Choice: American Literature* to read the poetry of Langston Hughes. Explain that one of the most prolific, original, and versatile writers of the Harlem Renaissance was Langston Hughes. Born in Joplin, Missouri, Hughes became a leading voice of the African American experience in the United States. In poems such as "The Negro Speaks of Rivers," he revealed a profound love of his heritage through deeply moving lyrics:

I've known rivers:
I've known rivers ancient as the world and older
than the flow of human blood in human veins.
My soul has grown deep like the rivers.

In the second stanza, Hughes alludes to rivers closely associated with the experiences of African Americans:

I bathed in the Euphrates . . . I built my hut near the Congo . . . I looked upon the Nile . . . I heard the singing of the Mississippi when Abe Lincoln went down to New Orleans. . . .

Hughes wrote this poem in the summer after graduating from high school. Its publication in *The Crisis,* the magazine of the National Association for the Advancement of Colored People (NAACP), brought early attention to Hughes and his writing. Hughes published his first collection of poetry, *The Weary Blues,* in 1926. In the title poem, he combined the musical rhythm of "low-down" blues with the spirit of the African American migrant in formal poetry. The innovation fused the blues to the African American experience.

★ACTIVITIES

Ask students the following questions, and then have them complete the activity below.

1. What do the rivers mentioned by Hughes symbolize? *(The rivers symbolize the path the lives of African Americans have followed—beginning with their pre-slavery ancestry to the freedom that flowed to them via Abe Lincoln.)*

2. Why do you suppose Hughes uses the pronoun "I" to narrate this poem? *(Hughes uses "I" to create a collective voice for African Americans.)*

3. **Writing Prompt:** Write a research paper about one of the following authors who contributed to the Harlem Renaissance and report your discoveries to the class: James Weldon Johnson, Constance Johnson, Zora Neale Hurston, Claude McKay, Jean Toomer, Countee Cullen.

Economic Shifts in the 1920s

★BACKGROUND

The enormous changes that occurred in the economy in the 1920s generated great wealth and brought prosperity to many Americans. Big businesses, such as the automobile industry, contributed to the reshaping of the post-war United States. Higher wages and shorter work-days resulted in a decade-long buying spree that kept the economy booming. Shifting from traditional attitudes of thrift and prudence, Americans in the 1920s placed their faith in pros-perity and enthusiastically accepted their new role as consumers. At the same time, the rise of mass production created more supply and reduced consumer costs. This formula reshaped the American economy and created, in effect, a second industrial revolution.

★STRATEGIES

Point out to students that perhaps no other author captures the extravagance of the 1920s like F. Scott Fitzgerald. In novels such as *Breakfast at Tiffany's, The Great Gatsby,* and *This Side of Paradise,* Fitzgerald cap-tures and condenses the attitudes that accompanied the varying degrees of wealth that existed during this era. Have students turn to page 652 in Glencoe Literature's *The Reader's Choice: American Literature* to read "The Bridal Party" by F. Scott Fitzgerald. Set in Paris, the narration focuses on Michael, the scorned lover of Car-oline Dandy, who is to be wed to the independently wealthy Hamilton Rutherford:

> **He had met Caroline Dandy when she was seven-teen, possessed her young heart all through her first season in New York, and then lost her, slowly, tragically, uselessly, because he had no money and could make no money. . . .**

The unexpected death of his grandfather and his subsequent inheritance renew Michael's fortitude to win Caroline:

> **"Well, I won't give up till the last moment," he whispered. "I've had all the bad luck so far, and maybe it's turned at last."**

Deciding to fight for the girl he thinks would love him were he not impoverished, he talks to Caroline without revealing his new wealth, and then, when he talks alone with Rutherford, finds that perhaps Caro-line really does love Rutherford:

> **She said, "Why should I be [nervous]? I've been after him for two years, and now I'm just happy, that's all."**

Just before the wedding, Fitzgerald brings the three-some together in the lobby of a hotel. Michael reveals that he has come into money, Rutherford reveals that he has lost his fortune to the crash, and Caroline reveals her true loyalties as she rushes into Rutherford's arms:

> **"Oh, darling," she cried, "what does it matter! It's better; I like it better, honestly I do! I want to start that way; I want to! Oh, please don't worry or be sad even for a minute!"**

Finally, Michael realizes that Caroline Dandy chose the man she wanted, and he rather effortlessly moves on:

> **[H]e walked forward to bid Hamilton and Caroline Rutherford good-bye.**

★ACTIVITIES

Ask students the following questions, and then have them complete the activity below.

1. Identify the central conflict and explain. *(The cen-tral conflict is internal. Michael has a difficult time reconciling himself to the fact that he wants a woman who does not want him. His willingness to accept his inheritance and his inability to earn money lead the reader to believe he has low self-esteem and a lack of ambition, both of which are internal conflicts.)*

2. In your opinion, did Caroline choose the right man? *(Students' answers may vary. Most will agree that she did choose the right man because Rutherford was optimistic about regaining his losses. He cared for her and she cared for him.)*

3. **Writing Prompt:** Rewrite a pivotal scene from Caroline or Rutherford's point of view.

The Great Depression

★BACKGROUND

During the Great Depression, families who could not pay their rent or mortgage lost their homes. In search of work or a slim chance at a better life, an army of homeless and jobless Americans began to wander around the country, walking, hitchhiking, or, most often, "riding the rails." Throughout the country, newly homeless people put up shacks on unused or public lands. Some Midwestern and Great Plains farmers managed to hold on to their land, but many had no chance. If their withered fields were mortgaged, they had to turn them over to the banks. Then, nearly penniless, many families packed their belongings into old cars or trucks and headed west, hoping for a better life in California. They usually found no better opportunities in California than spending a few days picking produce at rock-bottom wages. They lived in makeshift roadside camps and remained homeless and impoverished.

★STRATEGIES

Have students read "Breakfast" by John Steinbeck on page 798 in Glencoe Literature's *The Reader's Choice: American Literature*. Explain to students that one of John Steinbeck's four novels, *The Grapes of Wrath*, won a Pulitzer Prize for its depiction of human dignity in the face of injustice and depravity during the Depression years. The novel traces one family's journey from the Dust Bowl of Oklahoma to the rich, fertile farmland of the Salinas Valley in search of work and a new life.

Upon arriving in California, the Joads expect the supple land to yield its bounty to them. Instead, they join makeshift communities as the Joad men seek work, and they learn firsthand of the difficulties that humans sometimes face at the hands of those who are more powerful. While students may tend to think of life in such camps as unfavorable, Steinbeck creates for the reader a picture of hard-working people who survive the roughest of circumstances with humble pride. "Breakfast" was first written as a short story, but later became part of a chapter in *The Grapes of Wrath*. "Breakfast" is the story of an unnamed narrator who warmly recalls an early morning moment spent with an encamped family of farm laborers:

> **Then the tent flap jerked up and a young man came out and an older man followed him. . . . Together they stood looking quietly at the lightening east; they yawned together and looked at the light on the hill rims.**

Through the narrator's eyes, the reader views the situation of this family as beautiful, plentiful, and hopeful. Invited to share breakfast prepared by the younger man's nursing wife, the narrator describes the event:

> **We filled our plates, poured bacon gravy over our biscuits and sugared our coffee. . . . The young man said, "We've been eating good for twelve days." We all ate quickly, frantically, and refilled our plates and ate quickly again until we were full and warm. . . . The two men faced the east and their faces were lighted by the dawn, and I looked up for a moment and saw the image of the mountain and the light coming over it reflected in the older man's eyes.**

As the two men leave the camp for the fields, the narrator reflects upon the ability of hard-working people to create a content and peaceful life for themselves:

> **That's all. I know, of course, some of the reasons why it was pleasant. But there was some element of great beauty there that makes the rush of warmth when I think of it.**

★ACTIVITIES

Ask students the following questions, and then have them complete the activity below.

1. Describe the mood created in this selection. *(The mood is one of peace and harmony.)*

2. Explain how this mood is created. *(The vivid description of the sun rising and reflecting in the older and younger man contributes to the peaceful mood. The imagery of the young woman preparing a delicious breakfast over a camp stove, feeding her newborn baby, and eating with her men and a stranger they have welcomed creates a sense of harmony.)*

3. **Writing Prompt:** Write a personal narrative about a time you overcame an obstacle with dignity.

Franklin Roosevelt's New Way of Thinking

★BACKGROUND

On March 4, 1933, President Franklin D. Roosevelt and his advisers came into office bursting with ideas for recovery from the Great Depression. In Roosevelt's first 100 days in office, Congress passed 15 majors acts to meet the economic crisis. Together, these programs made up what would later be called the First New Deal.

Although the New Deal programs pumped money and jobs into the economy, they did not restore prosperity. Thus, in 1935 President Roosevelt launched the Second New Deal—another series of programs and reforms that he hoped would speed up the nation's recovery. One of the programs was the Works Progress Administration (WPA), which hired workers to construct highways, public buildings, parks, bridges, and airports. One section of the WPA was "Federal Number One," an agency that offered work to artists, musicians, theater people, and writers.

★STRATEGIES

James Baldwin grew up in Harlem during the economic hard times of the Great Depression. His own grandparents had been enslaved. Baldwin achieved fame as a writer, primarily for his 1953 novel *Go Tell It on the Mountain*. A Realist, Baldwin's writing exposed truths about the society in which African Americans were expected to live.

Have students read "The Rockpile" by James Baldwin on page 865 in Glencoe Literature's *The Reader's Choice: American Literature.* "The Rockpile" is set in the New York neighborhood of Harlem in the 1930s, the time and place of Baldwin's own youth. The third-person narration focuses first on John, the half brother of Roy. The father figure in the selection is Gabriel, a stern minister who reflects characteristics of Baldwin's own stepfather. Gabriel has dictated that the brothers must not leave the family apartment. When Roy sneaks from the fire escape, he is superficially wounded on a nearby rockpile. John and his mother, Elizabeth, both know there will be penance to pay when Gabriel arrives home. As expected, Gabriel first holds Elizabeth responsible for Roy's irresponsibility:

> **"You got a lot to say *now*," he said, "but I'll have *me* something to say in a minute. I'll be wanting to know when all this happened, what you was doing with your eyes *then*."**

Initially, Gabriel is angry toward Elizabeth for Roy's slight injury, and Elizabeth infers Gabriel's thoughts:

> **His eyes were struck alive, unmoving, blind with malevolence—she felt, like the pull of the earth at her feet, his longing to witness her perdition.**

> **Again, as though it might be propitiation, she moved the child in her arms. And at this his eyes changed, he looked at Elizabeth, the mother of his children, the helpmeet given by the Lord.**

As Gabriel becomes aware of the role Elizabeth plays in his life, his eyes change, and the future release of his anger is foreshadowed in the final passage of the story when Elizabeth directs John to pick Gabriel's lunchbox from the floor:

> **She heard, behind her, his [John] scrambling movement as he left the easy chair, the scrape and jangle of the lunchbox as he picked it up, bending his dark head near the toe of his father's heavy shoe.**

★ACTIVITIES

Ask students the following questions, and then have them complete the activity below.

1. What do you think the rockpile symbolizes? *(Answers will vary. Given the religious nature of the family and Gabriel's mandate that the boys are not to play there, the rockpile could symbolize "forbidden fruit" or something that is harmful or sinful.)*

2. In your opinion, what events do the final lines of the selection foreshadow? *(The lines suggest that violence is to come. The earlier references to Gabriel's hatred as well as the fear Elizabeth and John experience while waiting for Gabriel contribute to this idea.)*

3. **Writing Prompt:** Locate three Web sites that present a picture of Harlem during the Depression. Write a summary of the information that can be found at each site.

Jewish Persecution and Immigration Attempts

★BACKGROUND

Anti-Jewish violence erupted throughout Germany and Austria on November 9, 1938. That night came to be called *Kristallnacht,* or the "night of broken glass," because broken glass littered the streets afterward. When daylight came, more than 90 Jews lay dead, hundreds were badly injured, and thousands more were terrorized. The Nazis had forbidden police to interfere while roving bands of thugs destroyed 7,500 Jewish businesses and wrecked nearly 180 synagogues.

Kristallnacht and its aftermath marked a significant escalation in the Nazi policy of persecution against the Jews. Many Jews decided that it was time to leave and fled to the United States. Between 1933, when Hitler took power, and the start of World War II in 1939, some 350,000 Jews escaped Nazi-controlled Germany.

★STRATEGIES

Point out that in the early 1900s, more than two million Jews from Eastern Europe immigrated to America. A large concentration of Jewish immigrants settled on the Lower East Side of Manhattan, creating a vibrant Jewish subculture in New York City. During the years preceding World War II, many European Jews attempted to flee and reach their relatives in America. Ask students to read "The Magic Barrel" by Bernard Malamud on page 875 in Glencoe Literature's *The Reader's Choice: American Literature.* Explain that Malamud was the son of Russian Jewish immigrants who settled in New York's East Side. Malamud was the author of *The Natural,* the story of the rise and fall of a great baseball player, and also won acclaim as a writer of short stories.

Explain that "The Magic Barrel" is the story of Leo Finkle, an impoverished rabbinical student who has been studying at Yeshivah University in New York City and is about to graduate. Leo is told that marriage would improve his chances of winning a congregation, but he has no wifely prospects. He turns to a Jewish marriage broker, Pinye Salzman, who offers him several photographs of seemingly viable choices for matrimony. All are pulled from Salzman's "magic barrel" of photographs of women who are looking for husbands. Finkle agrees to meet one candidate. When the young woman asks him about his profession, Finkle realizes that Salzman had created false expectations in both of them:

> He stared at her. Then it came to him that she was talking not about Leo Finkle, but of a total stranger, some mystical figure, perhaps even passionate prophet that Salzman had dreamed up for her—no relation to the living or dead. Leo trembled with rage and weakness.

Finkle decides to seek love for himself and dismisses the marriage broker, who leaves Finkle an envelope of photographs of eligible women desiring marriage—just in case. When March arrives, Finkle is no closer to marriage. He opens the envelope left by Salzman and falls in love with a woman in a snapshot. He desperately hunts down Salzman, who states that the picture is of his own ungodly daughter and should not have been included with the other photographs. Finkle tries to forget Stella, but eventually concludes that to convert Stella to goodness would be to convert himself to God. Encouraged by this idea, he demands to meet Stella. Salzman arranges it, and Finkle rushes to meet Stella, who is smoking and wearing red shoes, as Salzman stands off chanting "prayers for the dead."

★ACTIVITIES

Ask students the following questions, and then have them complete the activity below.

1. Who or what might be symbolically referenced in Salzman's prayers? *(Answers will vary. Some possibilities include Stella's old life, Finkle's Jewish life, or Finkle's life without love.)*

2. What does Finkle learn from his interaction with Salzman? *(that his love for mankind—and, thereby, his love for God—is remote)*

3. **Writing Prompt:** Some critics argue that Salzman tricked Finkle into falling in love with Stella. Argue for or against this idea and support your points with details from the selection.

Aircraft and World War II

✪BACKGROUND

World War II spurred the rise of the wartime aircraft known as the bomber. Henry Ford, the tycoon of the automobile industry, launched an ambitious project when he offered to create an assembly line for the enormous B-24 bomber known as "the Liberator" at Willow Run Airport near Detroit. By the end of the war, the factory had built over 8,600 aircraft, an average of 1 plane every 103 minutes.

As the war progressed, President Roosevelt wanted to bomb Tokyo, but American planes could reach Tokyo only if an aircraft carrier brought them close enough to Japan. In early 1942, a military planner suggested replacing the usual carrier-based short-range bombers with long-range B-25 bombers that could attack from farther away. Although B-25s could take off from a carrier, they could not land on its short deck. After attacking Japan, they would have to land in China. President Roosevelt put Lieutenant Colonel James Doolittle in command of the mission. At the end of March, a crane loaded sixteen B-25s onto the aircraft carrier *Hornet*. On April 18, 1942, American bombs fell on Japan for the first time.

✪STRATEGIES

Have students turn to the poem "The Death of the Ball Turret Gunner" by Randall Jarrell on page 857 in Glencoe Literature's *The Reader's Choice: American Literature*. Before reading the poem, ask students to list the evolution of war weaponry, from the muskets used by the earliest American soldiers to the stealth fighters employed in the modern age. Instruct students to refer to their lists as they read the poem. Notice the "NOTE FROM THE AUTHOR" below the poem; ask students to cover this notice before reading the poem.

Pair students and ask them to read the poem again, noting any changes in their impressions and discussing their ideas concerning the narrator with one another. Read the poem a third time, this time aloud as a class. Discuss as a class the students' shared and individual impressions of the narrator. Finally, read the author's note, calling special attention to the description of the job of the ball turret gunner:

A ball turret was a plexiglass sphere set into the belly of a B-17 or B-24, and inhabited by two .50 caliber machine guns and one man, a short small man. When this gunner tracked with his machine guns a fighter attacking his bomber from below, he revolved with the turret. . . .

Lead students to recognize their reaction to the role this man played in World War II. While some students may be aware of the role of the ball turret gunner, others will be surprised and perhaps even appalled by the soldier's function, especially when they consider the apathy revealed in the last line:

When I died they washed me out of the turret with a hose.

Instruct students to use a Venn diagram to compare and contrast their interpretations of the poem before and after reading the author's note.

✪ACTIVITIES

Ask students the following questions, and then have them complete the activity below.

1. Did the author's note contribute to or detract from your interpretation of the poem? *(Answers will vary. Some students will say that the comparison to a mother's womb allowed them to visualize the ball turret gunner. Others may say that the comparison was stark and frightening, perhaps making the wartime contributions of some too realistic.)*

2. Randall Jarrell is noted as being a brutal literary critic as well as a forthright, impassioned poet. He was a member of the United States Air Force and witnessed firsthand the destructive impact war has on human lives. Explain the message that the last line of Jarrell's poem sends about war. *(The insinuation is that people can just be washed away. Perhaps the message is that human life is dispensable.)*

3. **Writing Prompt:** Write a poem in response to "The Death of the Ball Turret Gunner." Using first-person point of view, pretend to be the wife, mother, child, father, or sibling of the soldier. Include the emotions of the character you choose.

McCarthyism

✦BACKGROUND

Born in 1908 near Appleton, Wisconsin, Joseph R. McCarthy studied law and served in World War II before his first run for the Senate. McCarthy's 1946 political campaign sounded the keynote of his career. Without making any specific charges or offering any proof, McCarthy accused his opponent, Robert M. La Follette, Jr., of being "communistically inclined." Fear of communism, plus McCarthy's intense speeches, won him the election.

After the 1952 election gave the Republicans control of Congress, McCarthy became chairman of the Senate subcommittee on investigations. Using the power of his committee to force government officials to testify about alleged Communist influences, McCarthy turned the investigation into a witch hunt. His tactic of blackening reputations with vague and unfounded charges became known as McCarthyism.

In 1954 McCarthy began to look for Soviet spies in the United States Army. During weeks of televised Army-McCarthy hearings in the spring of 1954, millions of Americans watched McCarthy bully witnesses. Finally, army lawyer Joseph Welch confronted McCarthy and asked him, "Have you left no sense of decency?" Spectators cheered. Welch had said aloud what many Americans had been thinking. McCarthy lost the power to arouse fear.

✦STRATEGIES

Ask students to turn to page 912 in Glencoe Literature's *The Reader's Choice: American Literature* in preparation to read *The Crucible* by Arthur Miller. Ask students to recall information they learned during their earlier studies of the Puritans. Have students brainstorm a list of as many characteristics of the Puritan culture that they can recall. Then explain that this selection is set in 1692 near Salem, a small town in the Massachusetts Bay Colony that the Puritans founded in the early 1600s. Explain that in the late 1600s, English merchants settled in the town, many of whom did not share similar religious beliefs with the Puritans. As a result, Salem was divided into a farming village and a prosperous town. Eventually, the villagers formed their own church that was headed by the strict Reverend Samuel Parris, whose severity contributed to dissension among the villagers. During the winter of 1691–1692, several teenage girls in the community began behaving strangely. Their behavior ultimately led to mass hysteria, social and political repression, and accusations of untoward behavior in innocent people.

Before writing his play, Miller immersed himself in the history of the Salem Witch Trials and based all of the characters in his play on real people. Ironically, the atmosphere in Salem in the 1690s was a predecessor to the atmosphere in America during McCarthyism and the Red Scare. When *The Crucible* hit Broadway in 1953, its relevance to the current American political situation was clear, and the House Un-American Activities Committee investigated Arthur Miller, going so far as to deny his passport to travel abroad. As you read *The Crucible,* create a Venn diagram to compare and contrast the political climate of Salem in the 1690s to the political climate of America in the 1950s.

✦ACTIVITIES

Ask students the following questions, and then have them complete the activity below.

1. Discuss the universal notions presented in the play that allow people worldwide to identify with the story. *(Humans understand hysteria created by unjust governmental decrees, fears heightened by biased media coverage, and lives destroyed by false accusations.)*

2. Identify the mood of *The Crucible,* and then explain the impact of the setting on the mood. *(The mood is tense, frightening, and at times leaves the reader in a state of disbelief. The setting in the play is crucial to the mood because the Puritans were deeply religious and believed that the sins of one could wreak havoc on an entire community. Additionally, the Puritans believed in a physical manifestation of Satan as well as conversion to the dark side. Without these elements, the witch hunts never would have occurred.)*

3. **Writing Prompt:** Use the Venn diagram you created while reading the play to write an essay comparing and contrasting the witch hunts in Salem to the Red Scare in America.

The Rise of American Suburbs

★BACKGROUND

The 1950s saw a rapid increase in the suburbanization trend begun in the 1920s. Low interest rates, the federal government's support for housing loans, and improved and cheaper construction techniques all helped make this expansion possible. After World War II, seemingly endless housing developments began to encircle the nation's cities.

One of the earliest and best-known suburbs was Levittown, New York. The driving force behind this planned residential community was Bill Levitt, who mass-produced hundreds of simple and similar-looking homes on a 1,200-acre potato field 10 miles east of New York City. Between 1947 and 1951, thousands of families rushed to buy the inexpensive homes, and soon other Levittown-type communities rose in states such as New Jersey, Maryland, and Florida. Shopping centers with vast parking lots soon sprang up to serve the new suburban populations, while businesses and factories also began relocating to the suburbs—where many of their workers now lived.

★STRATEGIES

Have students turn to page 1047 in Glencoe Literature's *The Reader's Choice: American Literature* to read John Updike's short story entitled "Son." Explain that like most of Updike's stories, this story is set mainly in suburban America. The time frame, however, is somewhat different in that the events occur in 1973, 1949, 1913, and the 1880s as the narrators describe the generational father-son relationships of a family. While each portrait reflects the societal attitudes of the time, each also magnifies the strain sometimes created as teenage sons mature into adulthood.

The story opens with a father describing the teenage angst of his 16-year-old son who finds fault in various aspects of his family:

He would like to destroy us, for we are, variously, too fat, too jocular, too sloppy, too affectionate, too grotesque and heedless in our ways. His mother smokes too much. His younger brother chews with his mouth open. His older sister leaves unbuttoned the top button of her blouses. His younger sister tussles with the dogs, getting them overexcited, avoiding doing her homework.

And such disapproval of a teenage son for his family is replicated in the subsequent portraits. In 1949 the son is unhappy with the dominant/submissive husband-wife relationship of his parents; in 1913 the unhappy son must contribute financially to the family's coffer; and in the 1880s, the unhappy son is away at seminary, preparing for a vocation he later admits he was not "called" to enter. Updike prepares the reader for this theme in the opening paragraphs as the father states of his son:

He would be a better father than his father. But time has tricked him, has made him a son.

The theme is built through each portrait, finally bringing the reader back to the son of 1973:

As we [the family] huddle whispering about him, my son takes his revenge. In his room, he plays his guitar. He has greatly improved this winter; his hands getting bigger is the least of it. He has found in the guitar an escape. . . . The notes fall, so gently he bombs us, drops feathery notes down upon us, our visitor, our prisoner.

★ACTIVITIES

Ask students the following questions, and then have them complete the activity below.

1. What does the last line reveal about the narrator's attitude toward his son? (*The words show that he understands the young man's desire to be his own boss and to have more control of his world.*)

2. What is proven through the series of vignettes presented by Updike? (*Essentially, the vignettes show that although situations may change, a young man's struggle for his own identity is a necessary part of reaching adulthood.*)

3. **Writing Prompt:** Write about your own quest for individuality in a reflective essay.

The Cuban Missile Crisis

★ BACKGROUND

In 1962 a Cuban crisis developed. Over the summer, American intelligence agencies learned that Soviet technicians and equipment had arrived in Cuba and that military construction was in progress. Then, on October 22, President Kennedy announced on television that American spy planes had taken aerial photographs showing that the Soviet Union had placed long-range missiles in Cuba. Enemy missiles stationed so close to the United States posed a dangerous threat. Kennedy ordered a naval blockade to stop the Soviets from delivering more missiles, demanded that they dismantle existing missile sites, and warned that if any weapons were launched against the United States, he would respond against the Soviet Union.

Then, after a flurry of secret negotiations, the Soviet Union offered a deal. It would remove the missiles if the United States promised not to invade Cuba and to remove its missiles from Turkey near the Soviet border. As American officials considered the offer, letters and cables flew between the two leaders and their chief advisers. The reality was that neither Kennedy nor Khrushchev wanted World War III. On October 28, the leaders reached an agreement. Kennedy publicly agreed not to invade Cuba and privately agreed to remove the Turkish missiles; the Soviets agreed to remove their missiles from Cuba.

★ STRATEGIES

Explain that during the Cuban missile crisis, schoolchildren across America engaged in air raid drills in an attempt to prepare for a nuclear attack. Describe the drills that required students to file into hallways, away from doors and windows, and to crouch with their heads between their knees, often covered by a schoolbook. Other drills required students to crawl under their desks in an attempt to protect them from harm. Encourage your students to recognize the futility of such drills and to imagine living in such an atmosphere. Then have them imagine being a new immigrant to America and attempting to understand the simplest of American terms that are complicated by the vernacular that permeates a country's language during a crisis.

Explain to students that this is the situation in which we find the first-person narrator of Julia Alvarez's short story entitled "Snow" on page 1032 of Glencoe Literature's *The Reader's Choice: American Literature*. This is the story of Yolanda during her first year as an immigrant in an American school in New York City. Her attempts to learn the American language are complicated by the war terminology floating around her: "nuclear bomb, radioactive fallout, bomb shelter." Fortunately, her teacher, Sister Zoe, patiently works with her, even when Yolanda throws the class into panic as she mistakes the snow falling outside the classroom window for nuclear fallout:

> One morning as I sat at my desk daydreaming out the window, I saw dots in the air like the ones Sister Zoe had drawn—random at first, then lots and lots. I shrieked, "Bomb! Bomb!" Sister Zoe jerked around, her full black skirt ballooning as she hurried to my side. A few girls began to cry.
>
> But then Sister Zoe's shocked look faded. "Why, Yolanda dear, that's snow!" She laughed.

★ ACTIVITIES

Ask students the following questions, and then have them complete the activity below.

1. Explain the literary effect of Alvarez's use of first-person narration. *(The reader has insight to the fears and confusion experienced by the narrator, as well as her trust of her teacher.)*

2. How does this selection depict the atmosphere of the country during the Cuban missile crisis? *(This selection emphasizes how the crisis permeated American society. Immigrants who were just learning the language were also exposed to new terms such as* nuclear bomb *and* radioactive fallout. *Schoolchildren became accustomed to air raid drills and fantasized about the effects of nuclear fallout.)*

3. **Writing Prompt:** Work with a team to create a dictionary of at least 20 current terms that new immigrants to the United States may find confusing.

Dr. Martin Luther King, Jr.

✪BACKGROUND

In the 1960s, Martin Luther King, Jr., who had earned a Ph.D. in theology from Boston University, became a leader of the civil rights movement. He believed that the only moral way to end segregation and racism was through nonviolent passive resistance. King drew upon the philosophy and techniques of the Indian leader Mohandas Gandhi, who had used nonviolent resistance effectively in his struggle against the British in India. King encouraged his followers to disobey unjust laws. "An unjust law is no law at all," wrote St. Augustine, whom King cited often. King believed that public opinion would eventually force government officials to end segregation.

On the evening of April 4, 1968, as he stood on his hotel balcony in Memphis, Dr. King was assassinated by a sniper. Ironically, he had told a gathering at a local African American church just the previous night, "I've been to the mountaintop. . . . I've looked over and I've seen the Promised Land. I may not get there with you, but I want you to know tonight that we as a people will get to the Promised Land." Dr. King's assassination touched off both national mourning and riots in more than 100 cities. In the wake of Dr. King's death, Congress passed the Civil Rights Act of 1968. The act contained a fair housing provision, which outlawed discrimination in the sale and rental of housing, and gave the Justice Department authority to bring suits against such discrimination.

✪STRATEGIES

Instruct students to read the selection from *Stride Toward Freedom* by Dr. Martin Luther King, Jr., on page 892 in Glencoe Literature's *The Reader's Choice: American Literature*. Students should read to identify and explain what Dr. King calls the "three characteristic ways" oppressed people deal with their oppression. According to Dr. King, this is the first way people deal with oppression:

> **. . . acquiescence: the oppressed resign themselves to their doom. . . . [And] thereby become conditioned to it.**

Dr. King alludes to Moses attempting to lead the Israelites from Egypt, only to discover "that slaves do not always welcome their deliverers." Dr. King states:

> **A second way that oppressed people sometimes deal with oppression is to resort to physical violence and corroding hatred.**

King stresses the impractical and immoral nature of hatred, stating that "the old law of an eye for an eye leaves everybody blind." Finally, Dr. King states:

> **The third way open to oppressed people in their quest for freedom is the way of nonviolent resistance.**

Dr. King presents a balanced argument for choosing the third path, emphasizing "the principle of nonviolent resistance seeks to reconcile the truths of two opposites—acquiescence and violence—while avoiding the extremes and immoralities of both." Dr. King stresses that nonviolent resistance to injustice is "imperative in order to bring about ultimate community."

✪ACTIVITIES

Ask students the following questions, and then have them complete the activity below.

1. Analyze the structure of King's persuasive essay. *(King presented the purpose of his argument in the opening lines. He presented the two negative methods of dealing with oppression and then the third, preferred method for dealing with oppression. He then admonished African Americans through a series of logical reasons to employ nonviolent resistance when dealing with oppression.)*

2. How would the essay have been affected if the structure were altered? *(The current structure allowed King to end on a positive point. He dealt with the negative points early in the speech, using them to build toward and then prove his third major point. Altering the structure would have affected, perhaps negatively, the impact on his audience.)*

3. **Writing Prompt:** Write a response to King's argument, agreeing or disagreeing with his major points.

The Vietnam War

✪BACKGROUND

When American troops entered the Vietnam War in the spring of 1965, many Americans supported the military effort. As the war dragged on, however, public support began to dwindle. Suspicion of the government's truthfulness about the war was a significant reason. Throughout the early years of the war, the American commander in South Vietnam, General William Westmoreland, reported that the enemy was on the brink of defeat. In 1967 he confidently declared that the "enemy's hopes are bankrupt" and added, "we have reached an important point where the end begins to come into view."

Contradicting such reports were less optimistic media accounts, especially on television. Vietnam was the first "television war," with footage of combat appearing nightly on the evening news. Day after day, millions of families saw images of wounded and dead Americans and began to doubt government reports.

✪STRATEGIES

This activity will look at the war from two points of view—a soldier's mother and a soldier. Ask students to read the selection from "The Woman Warrior" by Maxine Hong Kingston on page 1036 in Glencoe Literature's *The Reader's Choice: American Literature.* Explain that this story is set in San Francisco in 1969 and focuses on Brave Orchid, the matriarch of a family of Chinese immigrants. Brave Orchid is sitting in the San Francisco International Airport awaiting her sister's arrival from China. As she sits, the reader is privy to some of her thoughts, including those about the soldiers in the airport awaiting their flight to Vietnam:

> They should have been crying hysterically on their way to Vietnam. "If I see one that looks Chinese," she thought, "I'll go over and give him some advice."

The sight of these soldiers leads Brave Orchid to ruminate about her own son's situation in Vietnam, and she reveals that "I told him to flee to Canada, but he wouldn't go." She sends positive thoughts toward her son, whom she believes to be in Da Nang.

Then have students read "Ambush" by Tim O'Brien on page 1063 to see the war from a soldier's perspective. O'Brien was drafted into the army in 1968. In Vietnam he became a sergeant who earned a Purple Heart. "Ambush" tells the fictionalized story of an American soldier who is charged with final watch while the second member of his two-man team sleeps. Surrounded by fog and mosquitoes, the soldier lines up and straightens the pins of his three grenades, preparing for the Vietcong he eventually spies walking up the trail. As the American lobs the grenade, he is "terrified. There were no thoughts about killing. The grenade was to make him go away." After the grenade detonates, killing the young Vietnamese operative, the soldier reveals his internal turmoil:

> It was not a matter of live or die. There was no real peril. Almost certainly the young man would have passed by. And it will always be that way.

The story emphasizes the struggle of the American soldier to come to terms with his actions as he plays his thoughts for the reader:

> I'll watch him walk toward me, . . . his head cocked to the side, and he'll pass within few yards of me and suddenly smile at some secret thought and then continue up the trail. . . .

✪ACTIVITIES

Ask students the following questions, and then have them complete the activity below.

1. Attempt to explain the dreamlike tone of "Ambush." *(Answers will vary. Perhaps the soldier wished that his killing of another human being had been a dream, emphasizing his personal struggle with the realities of the war.)*

2. Build a connection between the two selections. *(The soldier in "Ambush" was living the nightmare Brave Orchid was cognizant of in "The Woman Warrior.")*

3. **Writing Prompt:** Write a letter to the American soldier rationalizing his actions concerning the Vietnamese soldier.

Native Americans in the Twentieth Century

✪BACKGROUND

Native Americans in 1970 were one of the smallest minority groups, constituting less than 1 percent of the nation's population. The average annual family income of Native Americans was $1,000 less than that of African Americans. The Native American unemployment rate was 10 times the national rate. Joblessness was particularly high on reservation lands, where nearly half of all Native Americans lived. Most urban Native Americans suffered from discrimination and from limited education and training. The bleakest statistics of all showed that life expectancy among Native Americans was almost seven years below the national average. To improve conditions, many Native Americans began organizing in the late 1960s and 1970s. Documents such as the Declaration of Indian Purpose of 1961, the Indian Civil Rights Act of 1968, and the Indian Self-Determination and Educational Assistance Act of 1975 have contributed to the improvement of conditions for Native Americans.

✪STRATEGIES

Point out to students that Native Americans work diligently to maintain aspects of their native traditions and customs. Literature is one mode through which the Native American culture is preserved, and a rich and growing collection of literature embodies the values and tragic history of the Native American peoples. Ask students to read the poem "Speaking" by Simon J. Ortiz on page 1109 in Glencoe Literature's *The Reader's Choice: American Literature.* This poem emphasizes the importance of oral tradition to the Native American culture, which Simon says brings "a sense of cultural being, continuity, and identity" to Native Americans. "Speaking" supports this statement as a father carries his young son outdoors to commune with nature.

Ask students to then turn to page 1119 to read Leslie Marmon Silko's poem entitled "Prayer to the Pacific." Home for Silko is the Laguna Pueblo Reservation near Albuquerque, New Mexico, where she grew up in an environment rich with oral tradition. "Storytelling lies at the heart of the Pueblo people," she states, and Silko explores traditional themes in her writing. Rich with naturalistic imagery, "Prayer to the Pacific" relates a creation myth, stating that "thirty thousand years ago Indians came riding across the ocean carried by giant sea turtles." Turtles play an important role in the origin myths of the Pueblo Indians, just as other creatures or objects are crucial to the origin myths of other groups. While specific myths and customs may vary, respect for nature is a constant in Native American literature.

Finally, ask students to turn to page 1054 to read an excerpt from N. Scott Momaday's novel *The Way to Rainy Mountain.* Momaday is of Kiowa descent and is a noted novelist, poet, and teacher. The excerpt shifts from modern-day Oklahoma to the childhood of his grandmother and then to the more distant past, blending autobiographical accounts with history and culture. For example, of his grandmother he says: "When she was born, the Kiowas were living the last great moment of their history." He then continues to summarize aspects of Kiowa history: "Along the way the Kiowas were befriended by the Crows, who gave them culture and religion of the Plains." Momaday also embeds aspects of traditional myths: "According to their origin myth, they entered the world through a hollow log." Momaday's primary emphasis, however, is the importance of man's commune with nature and one another.

✪ACTIVITIES

Ask students the following questions, and then have them complete the activity below.

1. Describe the father and son's relationship in "Speaking." *(The father loves his son; the son seems comfortable with his father and trusts him. They appear as one when communing with nature.)*

2. What conclusions can you draw about the relationship of the Pueblo to nature based on "Prayer to the Pacific"? *(The Pueblo communed with nature and respected all aspects of nature.)*

3. **Writing Prompt:** Momaday writes about the historical events his grandmother witnessed. Pretend that you are one of the many historical figures you have studied in this course and write a first-person account of an event this figure witnessed.

Challenges to Traditional Values

✪ BACKGROUND

The 1960s protest and counterculture movements had an impact on society. The campaigns of the era, especially the women's movement, began to change how many women viewed their roles as wives and mothers. These changes in turn led to changes in family life. With women increasingly active outside the home, smaller families became the norm. The birthrate fell to an all-time low in 1976, and parents and their children began spending less time together. A greater number of families also split apart as the divorce rate doubled.

✪ STRATEGIES

Ask students to read "Rain Music" by Longhang Nguyen on page 1067 in Glencoe Literature's *The Reader's Choice: American Literature*. Explain to students the changes that occurred in family life and traditional values during the 1970s. Then explain that after the end of the Vietnam War, hundreds of thousands of Vietnamese refugees came to the United States. Many of these families maintained traditional Vietnamese customs and spoke their native language at home. The children of these families, however, attended American schools and found themselves torn between their own desires—often strongly influenced by American culture—and the requirements of their Vietnamese culture. "Rain Music" is the story of Linh, the beautiful and well-educated eldest daughter of a traditional Vietnamese couple. When relatives inquire if Linh will become a surgeon, her parents proudly indicate the possibility of such an event, but make their primary expectation very clear as Linh's mother describes Linh's "friend":

> **"He was even born in Vietnam! But he came over here with his family in 1975. He went to Harvard . . . on a full scholarship!"**
> **"A possible son-in-law?" they ask.**
> **[Linh's mother] shrugs and sighs. "That is up to God."**

Unbeknownst to Linh's parents, Linh has become very good friends with an American named David. One afternoon, Linh talks with her younger sister, the narrator of the story, and reveals that David kissed her.

> **"I was raging inside, screaming in my head, 'Why can't his fingers be brown like mine, be my brown? Why is his hair curly, not straight, like mine?' I saw brown pigments run across my eyes, all different colored browns. Those pigments keep us apart."**

The sister questions Linh about Thanh, the man her parents spoke of earlier. Linh states about him:

> **"He's so perfect for me, just perfect. It's like he stepped out of my story and came to life. We speak the same language and share the same past. Everything."**

And when the sister's poignant question is asked, "How does he make you feel?" the values that have been instilled in Linh become obvious in her answer:

> **"He will be my lifelong friend. He'll make a wonderful father. That's what a husband should be. Our children will know the culture and customs of our homeland. They'll speak Vietnamese and English, just like us."**

The sister is not satisfied with Linh's answer, but Linh has been taught to uphold the values of her family, and she will do so even if love is the price.

✪ ACTIVITIES

Ask students the following questions, and then have them complete the activity below.

1. Summarize the dilemma that Linh faced. *(She was the firstborn child of her parents and they groomed her to be a successful Vietnamese woman. To fall in love with and marry an American man would have brought great shame to her parents. She respected her parents enough to sacrifice her relationship with David for her relationship with them.)*

2. How was Linh's reference to "pigment" symbolic? *(The differences in pigmentation represented the differences in culture. If David and Linh shared a similar culture, their love would not have been a problem.)*

3. **Writing Prompt:** Write a dialogue that might occur between Linh and David as she tells him that they cannot have a romantic relationship.

Poverty Amid Prosperity

★BACKGROUND

The inauguration of Ronald Reagan introduced a decade that celebrated wealth. By late 1983, real estate and stock values soared. The new moneymakers were young, ambitious, and hardworking. They rewarded themselves with expensive stereo systems and luxury cars. The strong economic growth of the 1980s mostly benefited middle- and upper-class Americans, however.

★STRATEGIES

Have students read "Se me enchina el cuerpo al oír tu cuento . . ." by Norma Elia Cantu on page 1097 in Glencoe Literature's *The Reader's Choice: American Literature.* Point out that although the 1980s were a time of prosperity for the United States, many people in the country did not share in the wealth.

Poverty plagues strains of American subcultures, and migrant workers are one group suffering from stark poverty. While some of these migrant workers are illegal immigrants, most are not. In the United States, about 500,000 people work as migrant workers, traveling through the country harvesting crops. This selection is about a son of migrant workers. One day the young man graduates as the valedictorian of his class and the next day he is helping his family make their annual trip north to a new place of work. When they arrive at the turkey farm, the boss shows them where they are going to stay. Educated and able to speak English, the family looks to the young man to question the boss at the turkey farm about their living quarters:

"What's this?" you [the young man] ask.

"This is where you're gonna live."

Perplexed, you say, "But it looks like a chicken coop."

"It is, but it's not good enough for the chickens," the Anglo responds with a sneer.

Left with no choice, the women in the family attempt to make the chicken coop livable, while the father and son begin working:

Then the work, arduous and demeaning, begins. Working night shift after long days . . . plucking feathers, forcibly breeding the toms and hens, and your Dad ages from day to day before your very eyes.

When his father is nearly suffocated by plucked chicken feathers, the boy determines his family is at risk and quits, jeopardizing their earned wages. When the educated boy stops to talk to the bosses and returns with the wages the family is owed, his mother is proud yet fearful of the boy who "speaks the language of the bosses."

★ACTIVITIES

Ask students the following questions, and then have them complete the activity below.

1. What conclusions can you draw about the migrant workers who lived in an abandoned chicken coop, which the farmer said was "not good enough for the chickens"? *(Answers may vary. Students may note that the family was accustomed to living in squalor. They had no pride and would make the best of any situation.)*

2. Why is it important for the audience to know about the son's education? *(Education is empowering. The son felt he could take charge of the situation and collect the earned wages because he was educated. He could reason and argue with the bosses.)*

3. **Writing Prompt:** Develop a theory for improving the living and working conditions of migrant workers. Draft your proposal and then present it to the class.

The Future of the United States

★BACKGROUND

After a century that saw stunning breakthroughs in science and technology, but also devastating wars and unimaginable human cruelty, the world faced a new century and millennium. During the twentieth century, colonialism had been replaced with self-determination of nations. Democracy triumphed over Nazism and communism. Racial segregation—but not racism—ended in the United States. By 2001 the population of the United States exceeded 281 million. Almost 10 percent of the population was foreign-born. About 82 percent of Americans were white, 13 percent African American, 12 percent Hispanic, 4 percent Asian or Pacific Islanders, and 1 percent Native American.

The great prosperity that boosted middle- and upper-income families in the 1990s had not helped everyone. Almost 11 percent of American families still fell below the official poverty line in 2000. The challenge for the new century would be to not only maintain the gains of the past but also to achieve greater economic equity and fairness in the new millennium.

★STRATEGIES

As students study the final chapter of *The American Vision,* share with them the following poems. Explain that as they consider each poem, they should contemplate the reflection of America—past, present, and future—that each poem presents. Have students first read "Frederick Douglass" by Robert Hayden on page 1146 in Glencoe Literature's *The Reader's Choice: American Literature.* The opening lines address the quest for equality that permeates American history:

> **When it is finally ours, this freedom, this liberty, this beautiful and terrible thing, needful to man as air, usable as earth; . . .**

The author continues by imploring the reader to remember Douglass as one who paved the way for the struggle for freedom and equality:

> **. . . [Remember] not with statues' rhetoric, not with legends and poems and wreaths of bronze alone, but with the lives grown out of his life, the lives fleshing his dream of the beautiful, needful thing.**

Next, have students read "Weaver" by Sandra Maria Esteves on page 1153. Explain that weaving is a creative process used in many cultures throughout the world as well as in the United States. As they read this poem, have students consider the symbolic plea of the speaker:

> **Weave us a song of many threads. . . . Weave us a song for our bodies to sing a song of many threads that will dance with the colors of our people and cover us with the warmth of peace.**

Finally, have students read "#2 Memory" by Victor Hernandez Cruz on page 1150. Encourage students to consider the implications concerning history that are made in this poem, which consists of but one sentence:

> **You have to know what you once said Because it could travel in the air for years And return in different clothes And then you have to buy it.**

★ACTIVITIES

Ask students the following questions, and then have them complete the activity below.

1. State the relevance of each poem to American culture. *("Frederick Douglass" reminds Americans to continue to fight for equality and to remember those who instigated and continued the quest for equality. "Weaver" encourages Americans to come together, to appreciate the cultural differences of this eclectic country, and to live peaceably. "#2 Memory" encourages thoughtful action and speech.)*

2. Do the poets give sound advice? Explain your answer. *(Yes. The words of the poets are poignant, beautiful, and cautionary.)*

3. **Writing Prompt:** Write an original poem addressed to young Americans. In this poem, offer advice concerning an aspect of American history or culture.

Teacher Notes

Teacher Notes

Teacher Notes

Teacher Notes

Teacher Notes

Teacher Notes